THEN IT ~~C~~
LOUDER
TAP-TAP-TAP-TAP.

John sat bolt upright in his bed. He listened intently. He knew he was awake. It came again.

Tap-tap-tap-tap-tap-tap-tap.

It was more insistent this time. He strained to keep his eyes open. He searched the pitch-blackness of his room. It was coming from the window. He tried to close his eyes and go back to sleep, but the sound nagged at his mind.

Then it came again. Louder this time. *TAP-TAP-TAP-TAP.*

John peeled back the covers and slowly got out of bed. Cautiously, he walked over to the window. In one swift motion, he yanked on the cord of his blinds, lifting them up so they clattered and crunched to the top of the window. His breath caught in his throat. He jumped back, startled. He couldn't believe it. He couldn't believe what he saw.

ARE YOU AFRAID OF THE DARK?® novels

Available from MINSTREL Books

NICKELODEON®

Are You Afraid of the Dark?™

THE TALE OF THE
HORRIFYING HOCKEY TEAM

K.S. RODRIGUEZ

A MINSTREL® BOOK

Published by POCKET BOOKS
New York   London   Toronto   Sydney   Tokyo   Singapore

This book is a work of fiction. Names, characters, places and incidents are products of the author's imagination or are used fictitiously. Any resemblance to actual events or locales or persons, living or dead, is entirely coincidental.

A MINSTREL PAPERBACK *Original*

 A Minstrel Book published by
POCKET BOOKS, a division of Simon & Schuster Inc.
1230 Avenue of the Americas, New York, NY 10020

ISBN: 0-671-02517-1

First Minstrel Books printing January 1999

10 9 8 7 6 5 4 3 2

Cover art by Broeck Steadman

Printed in the U.S.A.

For John R. Squires and John A. Squires,
helpful hockey fans

THE TALE OF THE
HORRIFYING HOCKEY TEAM

PROLOGUE: THE MIDNIGHT SOCIETY

*Hey, what are you doing over there in the bushes?
Come over and sit by the fire with us.*

*What's the matter? Are you afraid? Don't be
scared, and don't worry—we're not ghosts or crim-
inals or performing some kind of scary secret rit-
ual. We're just a bunch of friends who like to get
together, tell stories . . . and scare the wits out of
one another.*

*Hey! Don't go away. I was just kidding . . . sort
of. My name is Frank, and we're the Midnight
Society. We do like to tell scary stories. And I
know it's dark out, and it's creepily quiet in these
woods. But there's nothing to be afraid of.*

*Nothing at all . . . unless you count what lurks
in the dark.*

1

Wait! Don't go back in the night alone. When it's this dark, it's better to be here with us, isn't it?

Do you like sports? Yeah? So do I, and so did a kid named John Stevenson. He was a sports fiend—played a sport for every season. Baseball in the spring, soccer in the summer, football in the fall.

But John's favorite—his absolute favorite—was hockey in the winter. I mean, if you asked John he would say he'd die *for hockey.*

He didn't realize how close he would come.

The only thing that John loved more than playing hockey was winning *a hockey game. And this season was the best ever in Hillville Middle School history. The Hillville Penguins, after sixteen undefeated games, won the district championship. And they rode the glory high, even after the season was over.*

Not that there's anything wrong with that. The Penguins deserved to win. They played hard and mighty. And John and his friends were a good bunch of kids. They just didn't know when to call it quits.

While the town pond was still frozen over, the boys would scrimmage after school, reliving the glory of a few weeks earlier, biding their time until the weather grew warmer and baseball got under way.

And while they played, day after day, they tried

to recapture the victory in their minds, not realizing that their hardest challenge was still to come. They didn't know that they had yet to meet their matches. And they didn't know that they were about to play the game of their lives—for their lives.

In a short week, John Stevenson and the Hillville Penguins would learn the real meaning of "stiff competition."

And they'd learn that maybe, just maybe, winning wasn't everything. . . .

Oh, I see you're interested now. I'm glad you stumbled onto us. We could use some new blood. . . .

Just kidding, again . . . sort of. Just sit back, relax, and listen, but never let your guard down. Submitted for the approval of the Midnight Society, I call this story . . . The Tale of the Horrifying Hockey Team.

CHAPTER
1

"Face off!" John Stevenson shouted as he burst out of the front doors of Hillville Middle School. Now that he was in eighth grade, he didn't have to worry about getting trampled at the end of the day. He ran after his best friends, Sanjay Patel and Steve Chiang, remembering what it was like to be a pip-squeak sixth-grader.

He was glad those days were over. He loved being top of the heap.

John let out a breath, blowing puffs of cold, frosty air. There wasn't a trace of spring in sight. "Perfect slap-shot weather," he said. "We'll fly on the ice today."

"No question," Steve agreed, pulling his knit hat lower and mashing down his straight black hair.

"Faster than a speeding bullet," Sanjay said in his best announcer voice, using his stick as a mock microphone. "It's a bird! It's a plane! It's a . . . hockey puck!"

Steve and John high-fived Sanjay and laughed as they yanked their gear bags over their shoulders.

Though the school hockey season was officially over, the boys enjoyed playing informal games at the town pond after school. They had all been part of the champion Hillville Penguins—and since the victory, they couldn't get enough of the game.

Before last year—when the Penguins had started to pick up steam—the hockey team had had a reputation for losing more games than they won. This year that had changed for good: Not only did they have an undefeated season, but they were also division champions, largely due to John.

No one could get a puck past "Steel Wall" Stevenson, as some of his teammates liked to call John. Coach Ramirez even said that John was perhaps the best goalie Hillville had ever seen.

Off the ice, John was a friendly, easygoing kid. But put him in front of a net and he changed. John became fierce; a veritable Incredible Hulk on the ice, staring opponents down with his grim determination, blocking every hole in the net.

John knew he had always had a strong competitive streak, but this year it was different. He felt invincible after winning the championship. He hadn't been used to winning before that. Now that he had tasted the thrill of victory, he wanted to win all the time. "Come spring, we'll be baseball division champs, too," he had boasted to his friends the other day. "And then we'll take the soccer title!"

But baseball and soccer were far from his mind at the moment. "Let's hurry!" John urged his two buddies, who were loping along at a leisurely pace. "I want to pick first this time. It's my turn."

The boys had an unwritten rule: They took turns playing captains, though Steve was their captain in school. And whoever got to the pond first, picked teams first.

The boys kept the pond games as simple as they could. Depending on how many players showed, they'd play two-on-two or three-on-three, with two goalies. They didn't use a referee; they didn't need one. They rarely got into disputes and liked to play without the worry of penalties. The boys wouldn't even time the game. They'd just play until dark, when it was time to head home for dinner.

As they continued up the hill to the pond, John could see the tall, bare trees sticking up like porcupine quills, surrounding the ice. The area was called Grant's Wood, and it stretched for miles and miles. John ran a hand through his hair. The reedy trees nearest the pond resembled his brown, spiky do.

Though John and his friends were familiar with the edge of the woods that bordered the pond, none of the boys had ventured deep into them. For one thing, a bear had been spotted in the area, and it was a prime hunting spot for other game. But the woods were considered to be so dense that even the most skilled woodsman would have a hard time finding his way out.

John and his friends had always heard stories about people who had been dumb enough to enter, never to be heard from again. Though John didn't know anyone personally, he knew endless tales of lost campers, ill-prepared hunters, and curious children.

John's dad had told him that most of those stories were made up. But one town tragedy was at the root of it all: Back in 1949, six Hillville Middle School boys had ventured into the woods on a dare and never returned. John thought it was creepy that that had happened in his own town—even if it was a long time ago.

As the pond came into full view, John could see some familiar faces standing by the edge of the ice: Paul Linder, Kevin Montague, Hector Ruiz, and Tiger Swensen. Paul was the other captain for the day. John was bummed that he wouldn't be able to pick first after all.

Looking closely, John saw that people were already playing on the ice. He glanced at his watch. There was no way they were that late. They had sprung out of the school practically at the sound of the bell.

John squinted at the group that was playing on the ice. He didn't recognize anyone. But he could clearly see the dazed expressions on his teammates' faces.

"Who are those guys on the ice?" Sanjay asked.

Steve shook his head.

John shrugged. "Let's find out," he said, as he began to trot over to join the group.

John could see the mystery team more clearly now. There were six guys on the ice: one goalie at either end, the others playing two-on-two. They seemed to be about the same age as John and his pals. But something about them was off. . . . John couldn't put his finger on it at first.

As he dropped his gear bag, Kevin Montague shot John a helpless look. "They were already playing when we got here," he said.

John regarded the team more closely. Their uniforms were strange—different from the oversized jerseys John was used to. They were the same colors as the Penguins'—blue and white—

9

but they seemed heavy and woolen, not to mention stained and moth-eaten.

Then there was the equipment—or lack thereof. These guys didn't have helmets and the goalies didn't even wear face masks. John mused that they must be kamikaze hockey players. Though John and his pals didn't play in full gear when they were at the pond, they did wear helmets and some of the padding. And he'd be disfigured for life if he didn't wear a face mask.

The mystery team did wear shin guards, but they seemed thin and clunky—made out of a strange, inflexible material. John even thought he saw newspapers stuck behind some of the shin guards.

Then there were the skates: All of them looked like they were blades nailed onto their grandfathers' shoes. And the sticks—they weren't sleek, curved, and well-kept, with brand names emblazoned on the sides. Not even the goalie sticks. They were all straight and flat, appearing homemade.

Not one player wore anything that resembled something John owned, or even had seen in sporting-goods stores or hockey magazines. "Guess they're using hand-me-downs," he remarked.

"But they're not playing like old-timers. These guys are good," Paul Linder answered reverently, as two more Penguins, Barry Sears and Pete Woo, sauntered over, their expressions curious, too.

Sanjay sat on a log and laced up his skates. He cupped his hands around his mouth. "Hey! Nice shot!" he called. "Where are you guys from?"

He didn't receive an answer. The team on the ice ignored him, grimly and intensely skating past, not uttering a word.

"Hey!" Sanjay called louder. "I said where are you guys from?"

Just then a player stopped short, grinding his skates into the ice so that the shavings sprayed Sanjay. The player's red hair was matted down from sweat, and even though his face had streams of sweat coming down, it wasn't red with exertion. His skin was as white as the cotton clouds overhead.

"We're from here. Right here," the player grunted. "And can't you see that we're playing a game?"

Sanjay was taken aback by the player's rudeness. "Uh—yeah," he said meekly. "I was just—" Before he could finish, the player skated away.

"They've got attitudes the size of Canada," Hector Ruiz said, popping open a bottle of water. "What's their problem?"

"Better yet, why are they playing on *our* pond?" John added.

And it was *their* pond, John felt. After each

game, the boys hauled buckets of water from Mr. Wilson's nearby farm to smooth out the ice. After every snowfall, they gathered to clear it off. The goals were even made out of leftover fencing from John's own yard.

Sanjay rose from the log and cleared his throat. "I'll give these guys one more chance to be civil," he said, then hollered, "Do you have any idea when you'll be finished?"

Another player stopped short at the edge of the pond, right in front of Sanjay. This one looked slightly older than the other boys, and he was huge. But like the red-haired kid, his skin was as pale as snow. "Didn't you hear what Red said," he snarled, jerking a thick finger toward Sanjay. "We're trying to play. If you want to have a tea social, go somewhere else." Then he spat on the ground, a ball of saliva just missing Sanjay's skate.

John's eyes widened, and he exchanged shocked glances with his teammates. Not only was that a disgusting and rude gesture, but they all knew what a neat-freak Sanjay was. If anyone wanted to tick him off, putting a bodily fluid anywhere near him was the trick.

Sanjay narrowed his dark eyes and stared the rude player down. Sanjay was fearless; he didn't care how big this guy was. But the huge player didn't move a muscle. His expression was stone cold and dead serious. Even scary, John thought.

12

Sanjay spoke again, with forced composure. "I asked you when you would be done with the pond," he said evenly.

"Never," the player answered gruffly. "It's our pond. And we're tired of you losers hogging it." Suddenly his teammates stopped playing and slowly gathered around him. Even though the Penguins outnumbered the strangers, John felt the power of six mean glares—and the stench of six sweaty guys in dirty old uniforms. He also felt a fight brewing.

Sanjay's mouth became a grim line. "We've been playing here for weeks at a time, every year, and we haven't seen you once," he challenged matter-of-factly.

The huge player puffed out his chest and hollered, "Get lost! We were here first. We don't need to explain ourselves to you." He leaned in close to Sanjay, their noses nearly touching.

Sanjay winced from his rancid breath. "Pew!" he said. "Can you say 'mouthwash'?"

The big guy shoved Sanjay.

John instantly leapt up. "Wait a minute!" he said, pushing the two boys apart. He was struck with an idea. "You can't play a decent game with only six guys. Why don't we play for the pond? If we win, we get pond dibs. If we lose, it's all yours." A little competition was certainly better than having a fight, John figured. Plus, as bonafide

13

champions, he was certain there was no chance of losing.

The huge guy turned to his teammates, who grumbled and nodded in agreement. "All right," he growled after a few seconds. "It's about time you played a real team instead of the Boy Scouts you beat for the championship."

That was a close one, John thought. Now he just hoped that there wouldn't be any brawls on the ice.

The big guy stared him right in the eye as he picked up his stick, chuckling ominously. "You'll be sorry," he said. "Dead sorry."

CHAPTER 2

While the Penguins quickly pulled on their skates, padding, and helmets, one of the goalies skated over. "Who's your captain?" he gruffly asked John. Not surprisingly, the kid had a long scar on his right cheek.

John thought of the famous player Gerry Cheevers, who used to draw stitches on his mask whenever he was hit in the face with a puck. This kid looked like him—but without a mask, and with a real scar. "I have an extra mask if you want," John offered, thinking of all the pucks he must have taken.

"I don't need a mask. Who's your captain?" Scarface asked more aggressively. His red scar stood out in contrast to his pale white skin.

John directed him over to Steve. These guys certainly weren't friendly, he observed, not to mention that they all could use a suntan—and a bath.

Steve introduced himself. "And you are?" he asked.

"Ready to play," the goalie barked.

"Okay then," Steve said, ditching all social effort. "I guess we need to go over some ground rules."

Scarface just nodded impatiently.

"Well," Steve continued, "it looks like you guys didn't bring any protective gear. So I guess it would be fair to say that there's no checking, and no slap shots."

"What?" the goalie asked. Then he broke into laughter, revealing a jack-o'-lantern smile, full of brown, rotted teeth. "This is ice hockey—not field hockey," he responded.

"Fine," Steve said, losing all patience. "If that's the way you want it. Everything goes. We play until dark." He checked his wristwatch. "Let's get started. We don't have a lot of time."

Six Penguins spread out on the ice while the rest remained on the sidelines. John took his position as goalie, Paul Linder skated to right wing, Sanjay took left wing, Steve skated over to center, and Kevin Montague and Barry Sears settled into defense. Usually, they didn't play with such formal positions at the pond, and they most likely wouldn't stick to them during play. But they wanted to show the mystery team that they meant business.

Hector Ruiz stood in the middle of the ice, ready to drop the puck. Steve crouched into ready position, glaring into the eyes of the kid called "Red."

John felt his adrenaline rise. He couldn't wait to wipe up the ice with these sick-looking, foul-smelling bozos.

"Face off!" Hector called as he dropped the puck and slid quickly out of the way. Steve fiercely thrust his stick out and pulled the puck back. He had possession.

But not for long. Just as he started to skate away, John saw Steve falter and trip. Judging from Steve's outraged glare—and Red's smirk as he stole the puck away—John could tell that Steve had been tripped on purpose.

So these guys played dirty, John thought. Since they didn't have refs, this was their cheap way of getting a win.

The Penguins didn't need to play dirty. They could beat any team, anytime. John remembered how the league president had even said he had never seen a better youth team, when he presented the boys with an enormous gold trophy for the school showcase. It was the school's treasure;

Principal Harris always beamed with pride when he passed by it.

So John was determined to show these so-called hockey players how a real championship team played the game. And he certainly wouldn't stoop to their level in the process—even if he had to put up with the bruising of his life.

Suddenly John snapped out of his dream world, realizing that Red was bearing down on him. John crouched, ready for anything.

His concentration focused like a microscope. He called out to the wings. "Sanjay! Watch on your right! Paul—there's an opening a mile wide!"

John's teammates always appreciated a vocal goalie, who pointed out things they couldn't see from their perspectives. They liked to joke that John had eyes all around his head, and that even when he was staring at the puck, he was aware of everything that was going on around him. "Steve! Keep an eye on the big guy!" he shouted out.

Red flat-passed to the big guy, who flipped to a kid whose uniform was so old and worn it was in tatters. He looked like he had crawled out of a paper shredder. John mentally nicknamed him "Raggedy Andy," like the doll.

As Andy prepared to shoot, John heard a voice behind him. "You can get anything past this

18

wimp! Wears a mask so he won't hurt his pretty face!" the voice taunted.

John was used to that kind of needling from the opposing team. Many teams used it as a strategy to distract the goalie's attention from the puck. But John wouldn't crack. *Call me whatever you want,* he silently challenged.

"That's a pretty uniform you're wearing. Did your mommy buy it for you?" came another gibe. But John didn't give it a second thought. He knew better than to get caught up in name-calling when the puck was at the net.

Raggedy Andy shot.

John threw out a padded arm.

Blocked. No problem.

Kevin picked up the puck from there, and sped down the ice like lightning. Kevin was the fastest kid on the team. His claim to fame was catching the other team off guard, stunning them with his quick action and clever fake-outs.

Kevin shot, but Scarface was quick. It was a nice save, John noticed. Scarface had deflected the puck without wincing, firing it right to a player on his team for a sweet pickup. John was inwardly amazed at how this kid had the nerve to play without a mask.

The game went on like that for what seemed like hours, without any score. Back and forth the boys skated: shooting, passing, defending their goals. But when John glanced at his watch, he noticed that only thirty minutes had gone by.

John was certainly as tired as if he had been playing for hours. This type of play was more strenuous than John and the boys were used to on the pond. It was even more intense than a real game, what with all the butt-endings, high-stickings, and charging. Even so, no one complained, and John knew why. Why let these creeps know they were getting to them?

After a few more laps across the pond, the captains called a time. Both teams huffed and puffed from all the exertion.

The Penguins gathered and sat on the logs on their side of the ice, while the other team retired to the side bordering the woods, to catch their breath.

John pulled off his mask. "Those guys are tough," he said. "I felt like I blocked twenty or thirty shots!"

Barry Sears wiped sweat off his brow. "They're fast and good," he said. "They don't need to play like they're playing," he added knowingly. He opened a water bottle and offered it to Steve. "I saw that wiseguy trip you, for starters."

Steve waved it off. "We'll win anyway. If they see that we're not flustered by that stuff they won't continue to play that way. Just watch," he said. "It's a big psych-out strategy."

20

"Well I for one am not offended by their playing," Paul cut in. "But I am offended by their odor. They're trying to stink us off the ice!"

Several guys nodded and laughed. It was true. John had noticed that their odor was . . . distinctive—like they hadn't showered in months, or just crawled out of a Dumpster full of fish heads.

"Probably another of their stupid tactics," Steve said. "We'll win despite the stench."

"If we ever score," Sanjay pointed out. "They've got a Steel Wall of their own over there."

"Yeah," John said. "I can't do all the work. You guys *have* to score. We are not giving up this pond to these creeps."

"Yeah!" "That's right!" "You said it!" the boys agreed, a new determination pumping them up.

"Break's over," Steve declared, noticing the other team milling back on the ice. "Let's get 'em! Let's score!" he clamored.

The Penguins cheered, then skated out to take their positions on the ice.

As John skated back to the goal, he noticed the cotton-white winter sun move lower into the sky. Night was going to fall pretty quickly, he figured. They had to score—and soon.

But by the last minutes of the game, when John nervously watched the sun go down, it looked as if no one was going to score. The players, skating

21

exhaustively back and forth, did all they could. The puck flew, bounced, and slid like a bullet. John and Scarface deflected them like superheroes—diving, stretching, throwing out arms, legs, and sticks in all directions.

The other team tripped, back-checked, elbowed, hooked, and pulled out every dirty trick in the book. But no one was hurt, and it just gave the Penguins more ire and more energy, and more determination to win.

Finally, after another save, John snapped the puck to Kevin, who pulled a classic decoy, faking the other team out by passing instead of making his trademark speed skate down the ice. Barry Sears received the pass and acted in an instant. Barry was known for his dead-accurate slap shots.

John cringed as he saw Barry hit the puck. It flew in the air, at rocket speed, just missing Scarface's head.

Scarface threw out an arm, but it was no use. He fell flat on the ice.

John thought he could feel the pond shake with the impact.

But the puck was in. It was nestled in the goal, finally at rest.

The Penguins had scored.

The boys let out a cheer while Scarface rose and snapped the puck to Hector. Hector stopped the puck with his skate and picked it up. "Only a few more minutes of play left," he said. "Soon we're not going to be able to see the puck."

"Just drop it!" one of the opposition hollered.

Hector dropped the puck. Red flipped it to a tall, skinny, blond kid who moved a quick break-out, getting out of his zone.

The blond kid passed to a short, squat kid who immediately shot it over to the huge kid.

The big guy received it right in front of John.

John gave him a wild look. There was no way he was going to let them score.

The big kid didn't even stop the puck. He was going for a one-timer, immediately pushing the puck so it flew high and straight.

John leapt. He couldn't reach the puck.

He panicked for a second, but then sighed with relief.

The puck flew even higher, missing the goal by a mile and flying into some bushes behind the pond.

The Penguins cheered. Night had fallen, and the game was officially over.

And the Penguins were victorious once again.

Before it had even sunken in, John felt himself being lifted into the air. Steve and Sanjay had hoisted him up in a victory cheer. "Penguins rule!" the boys shouted.

John thrust his gloved fist into the air, but put

it down when he noticed the other team slinking off the ice.

Sanjay and Steve lowered John, and Steve skated his way over to the other team, while the rest of the Penguins followed. "Hey, that was a great game," Steve said, always the diplomatic captain.

"You guys are tough," Hector added, sticking out a hand for a shake.

"Yeah, great game," John agreed, also offering a hand.

But the other team just glared and turned away, completely ignoring the Penguins' sportsmanlike gestures.

"That was cold," Paul said, mock-shivering.

"C'mon," Steve said, impatiently shaking his head. "These guys are nothing but a bunch of sore losers."

"Yeah," John agreed. "They have ice water in their veins."

The Penguins skated back over to their side of the pond. As they sat on the logs in the darkness, they pulled off their skates and padding and packed up their gear bags. The early evening breeze blew, sending chills and shivers up John's ungloved hands and arms.

The boys congratulated one another on quick reactions, clever plays, and numerous turnovers as Pete Woo and Tiger Swensen threw buckets of warm water over the pond to smooth out the grooves and holes from the wear and tear of the intense game. Each time they played, the boys took turns lugging buckets of hot water from the closest house to the pond.

As John packed up his bag, he couldn't get the weird opposition out of his mind. What was with them? Were they just a bunch of antisocial bullies from another town? Or some kind of freaky club? "I wonder where they're really from," John quietly remarked to no one in particular.

Sanjay answered, "They probably got kicked off a pond in their own town. . . . Or, better yet, they lost it to another team."

"I think these guys are from the North Pole," Kevin cracked. "Ice cold."

John laughed. He glanced across the pond to catch one last glimpse of the strange team.

They were gone. Vanished in the night, like thieves on the run.

And John got the uneasy feeling that he hadn't seen the last of them.

CHAPTER 3

"John! Wayne Gretzky just scored seven goals in a row! Hurry! Come look!"

The minute John walked through the front door, his seven-year-old brother, Marc, attacked him, leaping and tugging at his arm. John sighed and dumped his gear bag in the hall. He knew Marc wasn't talking about the real Wayne Gretzky; he was talking about a player on his hockey computer game.

"I'll bet my Wayne Gretzky can beat your Gordie Howe," Marc went on. "Gordie couldn't score seven G's in a row."

"Just because you name your players better than mine doesn't mean you're going to beat me, Shrimp," John said. No matter how exhausted

John was, Marc always begged him to play *Hockeymania* with him. "Plus, I'm tired. I'm going to take a *Hockeymania* break tonight. I've played all the hockey I could stand for today."

"But you didn't play with me last night either!" Marc protested. "What's the matter? Are you afraid you're going to lose?"

John laughed, "Now, you know that's ridiculous," he said.

"Prove it," Marc challenged, while their dad poked his head out of the kitchen.

"Dinner won't be ready for a while," Dad said. "Why don't you play a few with your brother? He's been waiting for you to come home all afternoon."

John rolled his eyes. "Okay," he said resignedly. He figured he'd get it over with. It was easier to play, kick Marc's butt, and listen to him cry when he lost than to put up with his nagging all night.

"Wait till you see," Marc said excitedly. "I put together a dream team."

John followed Marc into the family room and grabbed a joystick in front of the computer. Marc hit the Reset button. The players appeared on the screen.

"You changed the goalie," John noted. "Who is it now? Dominik Hasek? Or Tiny Thompson?"

"Neither," Marc answered. "It's John Stevenson. The best goalie in the world."

John felt a tug at his heart. Just when his brother was being the hugest pain in the world he turned into a normal—and pretty nice—little kid.

John ruffled Marc's sandy brown hair, noticing that he was wearing it just the way he did—short brown spikes sticking straight into the air. His brother was turning into a midget carbon copy of him. "I hope this Stevenson guy plays well for you," John said. "He looks like a wimp to me."

"No," Marc answered. "He's the best goalie ever. You'll never get anything past him. Not even Wayne Gretzky would. He's going to be famous someday."

John laughed, then started to play. All over again, he felt the familiar rush of adrenaline through his veins. He got a second wind. Excitement burned in his heart. His exhaustion was gone.

"Goal!" John called. "Take that, Stevenson, you sucker!" he yelled.

They continued playing until their father called them in for dinner. "Five–zip! I win—again!" John cried. He whooped and hollered and did a little dance that he knew annoyed his brother.

"It's not fair," Marc said, tears welling in his eyes. "You always win!"

28

John groaned in frustration. He didn't even know why he bothered playing with Marc. First of all, it was no challenge; John always creamed Marc. Then there was the crying. It was always the same story: John won, Marc cried.

"Hey, don't be a sore loser," John told Marc, who was wiping the tears out of his eyes. "I've had enough of those today."

"Good game today?" their father asked as they sat down at the table. He passed around a platter of veggie burgers. His dad had to be the busiest man alive, John thought. He was a doctor who ran his practice in the office attached to their house. Every night he cooked, no matter how late a patient might keep him. And, amazingly, he showed up at every single one of John's school games, no matter what season. John especially appreciated how his dad would enthusiastically cheer him on. Unfortunately, John couldn't say the same about some of his teammates' parents.

John nodded in response to his dad's question as he chewed. He was starving after the workout he'd had on the ice. "We played a pickup game with some other team," he said after he swallowed. "They were good players, but weird. Snubbed us when we went to shake their hands— really rude."

"They sound like a bunch of poor sports," Dad said as he wiped his mouth.

"Totally," John agreed.

"How could a good player be a poor sport?" Marc asked as he grabbed for another burger.

"Easy," Dad explained. "A poor sport can be a good player or a bad player. It's someone who misses the point of playing a game. Someone who's not out to have fun or just do the best he can do. It's someone who wants to win for all the wrong reasons, and someone who doesn't accept losing—or winning—gracefully."

"Like you, when you cry after you lose *Hockey-mania,*" John added.

"That's not true! I am not a poor sport!" Marc protested.

"Are too," John shot back. "Do you see Wayne Gretzky crying when he loses? Huh?"

Marc gave John a wounded look, then took another bite of his burger. John felt a pang of guilt, but he didn't want his brother to grow up to be a crybaby.

Dad caught John's eye, giving him a warning glance. "Don't forget that winners can be poor sports, too, son," he said.

John didn't understand why his dad was giving him that funny look. *Whatever,* he thought. When Dad got into lecture mode, John never understood half of what he was talking about. He was only trying to help Marc. What if Marc pulled his crying fit in front of the other kids? He'd end up being the last one chosen in gym class!

John chuckled to himself as he took another bite of his burger. *At least the losers at the pond today hadn't cried.*

John fell onto the bed like a dead man. He was so tired, and his muscles were so sore, he thought he'd never recover.

Images of the day's game played through his mind. Deflecting the pucks. Using every instinct and reflex he had. He remembered Barry's slap shot. Steve's face-offs with the redheaded kid. He thought about Sanjay's face when the big guy spit on the ground by his skate.

His mind raced. More images of the day flooded his brain. But soon he was interrupted by a tap on the door.

"Come in, Dad," John said. He knew it wasn't Marc because Marc never bothered to knock. Usually, he just threw open the door and ran in.

John's dad walked into the room and sat on the edge of the bed. He rubbed his head, patting down what little hair he had, which John knew meant his dad had something important to say.

"Your brother is still upset. . . ." Dad started gently.

"He's always upset," John answered.

Dad placed his hands on his knees. "I know it's

31

hard for you to understand," he went on. "And he shouldn't cry if he loses. But I think those are mostly tears of frustration. He's seven. He's no match for you."

"Hey," John pointed out. "In real sports he's always going to come against people who are bigger and better players. That's the way it is."

"But it's not real sports, John," Dad pressed. "It's only a game."

John didn't understand what his dad was getting at. "So, are you telling me that I shouldn't play with him anymore?"

"No." Dad shook his head. "That's not what I'm saying. All I'm saying is that you should let him have the joy of winning once in a while. . . ."

John opened his mouth in protest. "What? You think I should let him win? That's the lamest thing I ever heard!" John couldn't believe what he was hearing. "I'm not going to let him win just to make him happy! Losing helps him get better! It's not my fault he's such a crybaby!"

"Is it really such a big deal?" Dad looked John straight in the eye. "When you were seven do you think you really won at checkers that many times?"

John's eyes widened. "Yes!" he said, outraged. "Yes, I do!"

Dad just sighed and slowly nodded.

"Don't tell me—" John started. It couldn't be.

John used to be an excellent checkers player. He could beat anyone—even his grandfather. There was no way his dad let him win . . . was there?

Dad rose from the bed. "Listen," he said. "Just think about your brother's ego instead of your own once in a while. He tries hard." He walked over to the door. Before he flicked out the light, he gave John another meaningful look and said, "Be a good sport, John."

In the darkness, John plopped back down to his dead-man position. Good sport? He knew he was more than a good sport. Wasn't it good sportsmanship to even *play* with Marc after a totally exhausting *real* game? Some of John's friends wouldn't even give their brothers the time of day!

He was just trying to teach Marc how it is in the real world of sports, where fair is fair, even if you are playing against someone older or larger than you.

John rolled over and shut his eyes tight. Dad wasn't usually wrong. But this time, John knew Dad was way off the mark.

Right? he asked himself, just before he drifted into a deep sleep.

They were coming at him from all directions. Pucks. Everywhere. Right, left, up, down. John struggled, with all his might, to fight them off. They were coming at him fast as bullets.

But the pucks were going right through his gloves, right through his body. Strangely, he didn't feel anything. It was as if he were a ghost. Or some kind of character in a bizarre video game.

"Don't let us down, John!" his teammates were screaming. "We're the champs! Block those pucks!"

But as hard as he tried, there were too many.

Sweat poured down his brow, dripping onto the ground. He was exhausted. He couldn't take it anymore. Too many pucks.

"You let us down, John," a voice was saying. A very familiar voice. "We lost because of you. You couldn't handle the pressure. Now you have to pay."

The voice was clearer now. It was his own. But how could that be?

Suddenly, he felt like he was at his own execution, his back up against the net, tall, large shadows of faceless hockey players lining up against him. They drew out their sticks, wielding them menacingly.

"Now you're going to pay," the voice said again.

"Pay for what?" John asked. "I don't understand."

"You lost!" another voice screamed. "Don't you get it? You lost! The loser has to pay."

"Fire!" another loud voice called. The players began shooting pucks like crazy, one after another

34

after another. But this time they didn't go through him. John blocked them with every part of his body.

The pucks came too fast . . . too hard . . . he couldn't take it anymore. John just sank his shoulders and let them ricochet right off him. The sound of them pounding on his padding was like machine-gun fire.

Rat-a-tat-tat. Rat-a-tat-tat. Tap-tap-tap.

Tap-tap-tap.

John sat bolt upright in his bed.

Tap-tap-tap.

He listened intently. He knew he was awake.

It came again.

Tap-tap-tap-tap-tap-tap-tap.

It was more insistent this time. He strained to keep his eyes open. He searched the pitch-blackness of his room.

Nothing.

Again—*tap-tap-tap-tap-tap-tap-tap-tap-tap-tap*.

It was coming from the window.

What could it be? It couldn't be a tree. There were no tree branches by his first-floor window.

Maybe it was a bird? Whatever it was, it had woken him out of his nightmare. A nightmare about one of his biggest fears—losing, and having the team blame him. John shuddered at the memory.

He tried to close his eyes and go back to sleep, but the sound nagged at his mind.

Then it came again. Louder this time. *TAP-TAP-TAP-TAP.*

He had to investigate.

John peeled back the covers and slowly got out of bed. Cautiously, he walked over to the window.

In one swift motion, he yanked on the cord of his blinds, lifting them up so they clattered and crunched to the top of the window.

His breath caught in his throat.

He jumped back, startled.

He couldn't believe it.

He couldn't believe what he saw.

CHAPTER 4

There, at the window, stood Scarface—the maskless goalie from the pond the day before. He tapped insistently on the window with his stick.

John jerked his head back. He wanted to scream, but his vocal cords froze with fear.

He blinked. He rubbed his eyes. Was he absolutely sure he wasn't dreaming?

TAP-TAP-TAP.

No. He was wide awake.

He was awake enough to clearly see the scar that lined the young player's face: a jagged red river down his right cheek. It stood out like a tattoo on his white skin, which seemed even paler in the moonlight. And for the first time, John got a close look at his teeth. They looked like a rotten corn cob—yellow and brown and black. Above his sneer, dark half-moons ringed his eyes.

Frightened, John just stood and stared. This kid's face was as scary as any monster he'd seen on the *Creature Feature*. He wanted to run, but his feet felt like clay. He didn't know what to do. . . .

Suddenly he heard a muffled voice through the pane.

"Next game, we win, or else," the goalie threatened. "Or else!" he emphasized, making a cutting motion with his stick across his throat.

In a panic, John pulled the blind once more so that it clattered down. *Out of sight, out of mind,* he thought.

But he couldn't resist. He slowly lifted the blind again.

Just like at the pond: As quickly as he had appeared, Scarface was gone; a mere memory in the blackness of the night.

John had a hard time getting back to sleep that night. He lay awake, staring at his ceiling, his heart jumping at every little noise he heard.

John didn't know what to do. If he fell asleep again, he might have more nightmares about letting his team down. If he stayed awake, he might get visits from other frightening hockey players tapping at his window.

Questions swarmed John's mind. What was going

on? How did Scarface know where he lived? Had he followed John home? John wondered if any of the other guys were getting visitors in the night.

Was this all some kind of demented joke? And even if Scarface was serious, what in the world was he talking about? What "next game"?

As far as John was concerned, they'd won the pond rights fair and square, and he didn't expect to see any of those creeps ever again. He had played rough teams before, but there was something not quite right about this team. Something beyond their tattered looks and bad hygiene and rude combativeness. It was something eerie and chilling, and the visit in the night had clinched it.

John remembered the weird premonition he had had that day—the feeling about not seeing the last of them. John hoped that wasn't the case. He wanted things to get back to normal; he wanted to play the relaxed, fun, goofing-around games they usually played off-season.

To get his mind off the scare, John thought about the game. He thought about Barry's game-winning slap shot. He thought about all of the blocks and saves he had made. He remembered Steve's determined expression at each face-off. He conjured images of his teammates' red and sweaty faces. . . .

Then, finally, he fell back to sleep.

*   *   *

Morning came before he knew it. John could smell his dad's coffee brewing in the kitchen.

He sat up, exhausted. He had no idea how much—or how little—sleep he had gotten the night before. All he knew was that he felt like a zombie. A zombie with no sleep.

He stretched, threw off the covers, and stepped out of bed. Walking to the mirror, he peered at his reflection. Dark crescents hung under his eyes. Yep—he *looked* like a zombie, too. He was looking as good as old Scarface, he thought.

John shuddered at the thought of his late-night visitor. Did it really happen? Or was the whole night just one huge nightmare? He wasn't sure. His head was so clouded that he didn't know what was what anymore.

He moved to the window and pulled up the blind. The early morning sun streamed through the window. No Scarface in sight.

John squinted his eyes from the glare of the sun and looked out into the yard. The toolshed sat quaintly at one end of the yard; the swing set, where Marc liked to play pirate ship, glistened innocently with early morning dew. Dad's birdhouses were perched undisturbed in the trees, vacant because of the winter chill.

Too bad there was no snow on the ground, John thought. That way, he could have seen if there were any footprints from the night before. But everything seemed so normal. Maybe it had been a nightmare after all.

He yawned and stretched, then dragged himself out of his room to the kitchen.

Dad peeked up from the newspaper. "You're up bright and early today!" he said cheerfully.

"I couldn't sleep last night," John mumbled.

"Too much excitement at the pond yesterday?" Dad asked.

"Something like that," John answered.

Dad was a big morning conversationalist; John preferred to be mute. Dad continued with his usual morning banter. "Anything exciting happening today?"

John poured himself a glass of orange juice. "Pond game after school as usual," he responded through a gaping yawn.

"And how are your classes going?" Dad asked, cocking an eyebrow and taking a sip of coffee.

John shrugged. He got decent grades without trying too hard. He wasn't a straight-A student. But he figured he didn't have to get straight-A's if he was going to be a professional athlete someday anyway. And that was exactly what he planned to be.

"Guess that means status quo," Dad said as he flipped a page of the morning paper. "I hope there won't be any surprises on your report card. You know what that means," he warned.

"Yeah," John grumbled. "No sports."

Just then it hit him—there *was* something special going on today. John put his head in his hands and groaned. The one day that he looked like something out of a bad horror movie had to be yearbook picture day!

"What's the matter?" Dad asked, looking away from the paper.

"I just remembered—it's picture day," John said. "And I didn't sleep at all last night." Every year it was the same story. Last year it was a zit. The year before a bad haircut. When would it ever end?

"You look fine, son," Dad said. "You'll come out fine. Wear a bright color—it will make you look less tired."

John grunted in response as Marc came bounding into the kitchen. It seemed that he ran, bounced, or jumped wherever he went. John didn't know how anyone could have so much energy first thing in the morning.

John wondered if Marc had heard anything last night. "I guess you had a good night's sleep," he said casually.

"Yeah," Marc said, throwing open the refrigerator door.

"You didn't hear any . . . anything in the middle of the night?" John asked.

"No," Marc answered, shoving a bagel halfway

in his mouth and plopping down at the kitchen table.

Dad peered over his paper and eyed John curiously. "Something keep you up last night?" he asked.

"I thought I heard something," John hedged, "and then I couldn't go back to sleep."

John realized that if there had been someone outside, Marc would still be shrieking this morning. No doubt, then—the visit last night was definitely a dream. John frequently had weird dreams when he overexerted himself, or when he was overtired. And last night he was both.

John laughed to himself as he got up from the table and strolled back to his bedroom to get ready. How could he be so stupid as to think it was real?

CHAPTER 5

Flash! The light nearly blinded John as he had his picture taken.

The photographer came out from behind the camera and turned John's head slightly. She brushed some hair out of his face. "Why don't you try smiling for these few?" she asked sweetly.

But John didn't feel like smiling. It was the end of a long day, and he wanted to go home and crawl into bed.

Flash! came the light again. And again. "One more," the perky photographer sang.

"Hey! Why don't you wear your goalie mask?" Steve Chiang called from the doorway. "It at least partially covers your ugly face!"

John laughed, and the photographer snapped another picture. "Great!" she said. "That one's a keeper." She took some film out of the camera. "Okay, you're sprung," she told him.

John leapt off the stool and immediately pulled off the dumb blue sweater he'd worn for the picture. He didn't understand the point of a yearbook, anyway. He just didn't get excited about poring over pictures like his neighbor, Robbie Kaplan, did.

Robbie was the head of the yearbook committee. He always snapped pictures at the sporting events, making sure to include his old friend John.

As John stepped into the hallway, he thought about Robbie. He hadn't seen him in a while. He wondered how he was doing. They didn't get to hang out much anymore. Robbie wasn't into sports; in fact he was a classic couch potato, and though he was a nice kid who had a sick sense of humor that John admired, they didn't seem to have much in common anymore.

Sanjay and Steve were waiting in the hall for John, and they quickly followed him to his locker. John definitely had a lot in common with them— they were as sports-crazy as John. John grabbed his jacket and his gear bag and thought about how fortunate he was to have two best friends like Sanjay and Steve.

45

"Too bad your name comes at the end of the alphabet, or we would have gotten started a lot sooner," Steve said as they pushed open the doors and trotted outside, embarking on another trek to the pond. "I guess I don't have any hope of picking first today."

"Let's hurry, then." John jogged ahead of Steve, his gear bag bouncing up and down on his back. "But if we have unexpected visitors again today then nobody will get to pick," he said.

Sanjay laughed. "I don't think those losers are going to be coming back for more. What makes you think they will?"

John shrugged. "I don't," he said, remembering his dream from the night before. But he couldn't help asking, "I mean, have any of those guys tried to . . . contact you? You know, to play another game?"

"No," Steve said. "I mean, we didn't exactly introduce ourselves and exchange phone numbers," he said laughing.

"Yeah, right," John said. "Dumb question."

They jogged up the hill and when the pond came into view, the three boys stopped short. They were the first Penguins at the pond.

But they weren't alone.

The team from yesterday stood in a menacing cluster in the middle of the frozen pond. They looked like a bunch of scarecrows—ragged and wan, dark circles under their eyes, holes in their mouths where teeth should be.

It was strange, John thought. They were definitely about the same age as John and his friends. But they seemed older—in a different way from age. John couldn't quite figure it out.

"Hey!" Steve shouted, throwing down his bag when they reached the pond. He marched over to the edge. "We won this pond fair and square yesterday! What are you doing here?"

"We want a rematch," Scarface said flatly.

John shuddered at his words, and especially at his dead, mean glare. He seemed to be staring right through Steve, directly at John.

"Did you forget that we made a deal?" Steve reminded them. "This is our pond. We won. You lost. A deal is a deal."

Tiger Swensen, Barry Sears, and Hector Ruiz came up behind Steve. "What's going on?" Tiger asked.

"What, these chumps want more?" Barry mocked.

"Well, since it is *our* pond I guess *we* decide if we want to play you again," Steve said.

"We want a rematch," Scarface repeated.

"I don't know if we want to play you losers again," Steve said coyly as the last of the Penguins—Paul Linder, Kevin Montague, and Pete

Woo—arrived. "What do you think, guys? Should we kick their butts again or not?"

Scarface walked right up to John. He stared him straight in the eyes. "I want you to decide. Do we play again or don't we?"

John was up to the challenge. These guys really got his goat. He had no problem showing them who was boss one more time. "We play!" John said.

The rest of the Penguins cheered. "Same stakes," Scarface added. "The pond. If you lose, you stay away."

"Fine," John agreed. "Let's see if you can stick to the deal this time."

He joined the rest of the Penguins, who were suiting up for the game. These guys were certainly relentless, he thought. But he had to admit, it made things a little more interesting than usual.

As John pulled on his gloves, he decided to feel out the rest of his teammates. Not that he actually believed that his nightmare was real . . . he just wanted to make sure. "I am wiped. I had the worst sleep last night," he mentioned, carefully checking his teammates' expressions.

"You're kidding," Barry said. "After the game yesterday, I was so tired I slept like a rock."

"Me, too," Tiger added. "I thought I'd never get up this morning."

"Let's go!" Steve said, antsy to get the game

started. "Let's teach these guys a lesson one more time—I guess they didn't quite understand it yesterday."

"Yeah," Paul cracked. "I think they're a little slow."

The Penguins laughed as they skated to their positions. John laughed, too, though he was a little uneasy with Scarface's glare burning through him.

"Face off!" Tiger called, dropping the puck this time.

The game was on. John thought he had never seen Steve's face look so fierce.

The opposition took control of the puck first. The puck darted around the ice. Red passed to the big guy. The big guy flipped it back to Red. In a second, the puck was near.

John was ready. "Where's the defense!" he called out. "Quick! We need defense!"

Come on, make my day, John thought as Red closed in on the net. Red passed it to the big guy again. They continued, back and forth, making John dance. But John didn't mind dancing. He'd give them a chorus line if they wanted. He wasn't letting that puck through.

He zeroed in on the puck. But then John felt a presence behind him. Whoever it was felt a little close—like he was right in the crease. But John didn't pay him too much attention. If he was in

49

the crease, surely one of his teammates would have pointed it out. Whoever it was was trying out some kind of distraction strategy, for sure. John ignored him and continued to concentrate on the puck.

John stared at the puck as it slid hypnotically back and forth, back and forth, back and forth.

"You better listen," a voice said quietly. It came from the guy who was behind him. "We win or else," the player hissed, practically tickling his ear. "Understand? Or else!"

John whipped his head around. The tall, skinny, blond kid—so blond his hair was nearly white—laughed, baring big, yellow skeleton teeth.

That's when it happened.

In that split second, the puck broke through the Steel Wall.

John collapsed on the ice in a last-ditch attempt to thwart the goal. But he knew it was no use. He heard the cheers of the opposite team. He saw the disappointed faces of his teammates. It was in.

John was furious. These guys were playing the ultimate game of intimidation. The utmost head-game strategy. They probably did send the goalie to his house last night. They probably knew that the only way to break his concentration was to scare the living daylights out of him in the middle of the night.

Steve came to a stop in front of John and helped him up. "Are you okay, man?" he asked.

"I'm fine," John answered.

"If you're tired I could sub you," Steve offered. "Just say the word."

John shook his head, determined. There was no way he was going to get pulled. He was going to play this game to the end.

"That's just one!" John shouted. "There won't be others."

"That's what you think," the skeleton-blond rasped. He let out a sinister laugh.

John ignored him. He'd show them now. He wasn't going to fall for any of their tricks ever again.

The rest of the game, John's concentration didn't waver once—even though he was feeling really tired. He blocked every shot that came his way. He pictured his body to be bigger, thicker than it was. He imagined that it plugged every hole in the net.

It worked. Nothing got by him this time.

He thought about the opposing team and their stupid intimidation tactics. They probably met last night, coming up with ways to get to the cracker-jack goalie on the Penguins. *"I know,"* one of them must have said. *"We'll wake him up in the middle of the night, so he can't get back to sleep,*

51

and we'll scare him. And if he isn't scared, at least he'll be tired. . . ."

John imagined them laughing, proud of themselves for dreaming up the perfect plan.

Well, he was on to them now.

John drew his attention back to the game. Darkness was about to fall and they were tied at one–one. Sanjay tied the game when he had tipped one in from an awesome assist from Paul.

As the sun sank into the sky, the mystery team started to scramble, and again played rough. John didn't know where they got the nerve. It wasn't like they invested in any protective equipment overnight. John thought about his father's mini-lecture from the previous night. Talk about poor sports. If his father saw these guys, he'd put John in the good-sport hall of fame.

But the rough stuff didn't make any difference. The Penguins held them until the end.

John focused his attention back on the game, back on the puck. Barry Sears had the puck and was skating fast toward the opposite goal. A short, squat opponent checked him. Suddenly Barry was doubled over.

He gasped for air. Play stopped.

"What happened?" Steve asked Barry as he sped over. "Are you all right?"

Barry sucked in wind. He lifted his head and glared at the squat player. "I—I," he panted,

"I feel like someone . . . punched me in the stomach."

Steve and the rest of the players turned to the short kid. The squat player held up his hands. "I was merely checking him," he said without a lot of emotion. "I didn't punch him."

"I didn't see him . . . I just felt it . . . it seemed to come out of nowhere . . . this pain," Barry continued, breathless. Sanjay escorted him off the ice. Pete Woo subbed for him.

The game went back into play. John glanced at the sky. It was getting darker, and harder to see.

Paul Linder dropped the puck this time. Another face-off.

Steve took possession. He zoomed the puck over to Sanjay, who quickly passed to Hector.

With a quick flick of his wrist, Hector shot the puck. He didn't waste time. Raggedy Andy was right by his side in defense.

The shot was blocked. "Ow!" Hector hollered.

"What now?" Steve asked, exasperated. He called a time. "What's wrong?"

"My head . . ." Hector said in agony, holding both hands to his head. "It feels like it's going to explode. . . ."

"You guys seem to be pretty delicate," Scarface chimed in with a nasty chuckle. "Even with all that outer-space padding."

Ignoring the remark, Hector skated to the sidelines. Tiger subbed for him, and the boys got immediately back into play.

Another face-off. Kevin Montague took the puck. He sped like lightning to the goal, carefully handling the puck. But he was going so fast, that he sped past the goal—with the puck. Now he had to turn around.

John knew that to the opposing team, it looked as if Kevin had misjudged his speed. But he knew better. Kevin was famous for his decoys; he was the best faker in the league. John was sure Kevin had a plan up his sleeve.

And he did. On his way back around the net, Kevin crouched as if he was going to pass to a well-positioned Tiger. But he didn't pass the puck at all. Instead, barely noticeably, Kevin tipped the puck right into the net.

It was a brilliant, game-winning move. The Penguins cheered. It was two–one, and dusk had arrived.

John lifted his stick in victory. "Wahooo!" he hollered. The Penguins piled together in the middle of the ice. Another great game. Another victory.

John high-fived Kevin. "You are hot, man," he said triumphantly.

"Should we even bother congratulating them?" Paul asked loudly. "Maybe we should invite them to our victory party?"

"Don't bother," Scarface rasped. "We'll be back."

John laughed. "Sure! Keep coming back! We like to win! It feels so good. You're welcome any time," he taunted.

Scarface cocked an eyebrow in interest. "Is that another challenge, or do you just like to hear yourself crow?"

"As long as you keep showing up, we'll be happy to whoop you," John said. "That's a promise."

"Three cheers for Kevin!" Sanjay hollered. He started a chant. "Kev-in. Kev-in. Kev-in."

Sanjay lifted Kevin's arm, like he was a boxing champion.

John saw Scarface shoot Kevin a deadly glance before he turned and walked away to join the rest of his team.

"Aaaaah!" Kevin wailed. He jerked his arm down and grabbed his hand in pain. "My hand!"

The Penguins gathered around Kevin to see what the problem was.

"My hand," he wailed. "It hurts. I can't move it—"

"What in the world is happening?" Steve shouted. "Something crazy is going on!"

John picked up Kevin's hand in his, while Kevin continued to wail in pain. It was twisted and bent, like a bird's claw.

"Take it easy," Sanjay soothed. "It's probably frostbite. Let's get you home, and you'll be okay."

Quickly, John turned his head to the mystery team's side of the pond.

Like yesterday, they were gone. And somehow he knew they were responsible for today's mysterious injuries.

CHAPTER 6

John's body ached as he made his way home that night. Between his lack of sleep and furious game playing, he was beat. He felt like something from *Night of the Living Dead*.

As he dragged his feet down the street, he heard a voice calling him.

"Dude! What's up!"

John could just make out Robbie Kaplan's distinctive black, curly hair under his porch light across the street. John waved.

"How's it going?" John asked as he strolled over in Robbie's direction. He felt bad that they didn't hang out much anymore. But they just had different interests nowadays.

Robbie put down the comic book he was reading. "It's going pretty well," he answered. "Where are you coming from? You look like you belong on a stretcher."

"Pickup hockey game on the pond," John replied. "There's this weird group of guys who've been showing up for the past two days, challenging us. They're really good, but really rough—and strange," John told him. "I like to call them the mystery team."

"Cool!" Robbie said. "Where are they from?"

"That's the weird part," John answered, as he lowered himself onto the steps next to Robbie. "We have no idea. . . . Spooky bunch of guys. You have to see them to believe them," he said thoughtfully.

"So, you wanna hang out tonight? Watch some movies or something?" Robbie asked. "It's been a while. . . ."

"I'd love to, but I'm wiped," John said as he stood to go. "From the game today."

Robbie looked slightly disappointed. "What about tomorrow, after school, then? I have some great new cool CD-ROMs—"

"Sorry," John said, cutting him off. "I'm playing hockey at the pond tomorrow. But we'll hang some other time."

John gave Robbie a quick wave, and started to go.

"Wait!" Robbie said. "I need to take some

photos for the yearbook. Maybe I can come to the pond tomorrow and snap a few."

"That would be great," John agreed. Then he laughed. "If the other team doesn't break the camera. They are *U-G-L-Y.*"

"Okay, great," Robbie said. "I'll swing by after school."

"Hey," John said, stopping and suddenly reminiscing. "Remember when we were little kids, and we'd shoot tennis balls up against your garage door?"

Robbie laughed. "Yeah," he said. "I remember."

"What happened? Why don't you like sports anymore?" John asked curiously. They had both gone in such different directions since then.

"Well, I was never really a superstar athlete," Robbie said.

"But you weren't bad," John cut in. "You could hold your own."

Robbie waved a careless hand. "I don't mind goofing around, having fun. I just hate the organized thing. And the competing . . . once you get into stats and wins and losses and coaches barking orders at you and all the pressure . . . I don't know . . . it just doesn't seem fun to me."

John nodded, feigning understanding. What in the world did Robbie mean? That was the fun part of sports! Winning the game! Having the best batting average! Grace under pressure! Robbie just didn't get it.

"All right, then," John said as he stiffly strolled away, still hurting from the game. "I'll see you tomorrow—at the pond."

"I'll try to get your best side!" Robbie called after him.

Marc was waiting for John the second he walked through the door. *Sometimes,* John mused, *Marc was more like a hyperactive pet than an over-eager little brother.*

"I totally can't tonight, champ," John said gently. "I didn't get any sleep last night. I'm really tired."

"Please," Marc begged.

John shook his head. "And my body is sore all over. I'm way too beat, plus I have homework to do."

Marc looked disappointed, but he didn't press. "Okay," he said.

John felt a little bad for Marc, who always seemed excited when John got home. But then again, he didn't feel like the whole *Hockeymania* routine, and he certainly couldn't deal with Dad and his postgame lecture about computer-game etiquette.

"Tomorrow we'll play," John assured his little brother. "I promise, okay?"

Marc nodded, then ran off to challenge Dad.

John went to his room and collapsed on his bed. He opened up his algebra book, but soon found his eyes closing.

He snapped his eyes open when he heard a tapping at his door.

It was his dad. "Dinner will be ready in a few, Sport," he whispered. "If you want to nap, I'll save you a plate."

"Sounds good, Dad," John said wearily.

"Rough game again?" Dad added.

"That's a nice way of putting it," John answered, then closed his eyes again as his father quickly shut the door.

What a day it had been. He reflected on the game, and the sudden weird afflictions that had taken over Barry, Hector, and Kevin at the end. What was up with that? It was spooky, and John had a nagging feeling that the opposition had something to do with it. But how? Did they cast spells or something? John scoffed at his own silliness. They were all just eerie coincidences.

They had to be. He could find no other explanation.

John leapt off his porch steps the next morning, ready to walk to school. It was a mild winter morning, and everything seemed peaceful. Today he had so much energy he felt like running to school. The night before he had finally gotten some sleep—without any wacky nightmares or visitors in the night.

He took a bite from the apple he grabbed on his way out of the house. He figured he'd better pick up the pace because he was running late. Last night he had slept straight through dinner. His dad didn't seem too happy about it. "Take it easy at the pond today," Dad had said before he left for work. "Give yourself a break—you play too hard."

But that was the way he always played, John reasoned. It was a typical Dad thing to say. Dad loved being a spectator; he was John's number-one fan. But he wasn't much of an athlete, and he didn't understand what it was like at all.

If you weren't going to play hard, what was the point of playing at all? That was John's philosophy.

As he walked down the drive, John's eyes fell on Robbie's house and he remembered their conversation from the night before. Robbie was another one who missed the point, John thought. What was all that stuff about sports not being fun when you're competing?

As he stretched out an arm and dragged his finger along the bushes, he heard a sudden rustling up ahead.

He stopped.

The rustling stopped.

He slowly continued walking.

The rustling started again.

Suddenly John jumped back. The next thing he knew, he was staring into a battered old goalie's mask—the antique kind that Jason used to wear in the *Friday the 13th* movies.

"Rematch today," a voice from beneath the mask rasped. "You lose this time or else!"

John stared at the mask, then broke out laughing. It had to be Scarface. "So you won't wear a mask during the game, but for scaring me, it's a must." He laughed at his own joke and then paused to catch his breath. "Where did you dig that old thing up anyway?"

"This is no joke," the voice hissed. "If we don't win, you will be very, very sorry. Yesterday was just an example of what we can do to you. . . ."

John laughed again. "Oh, you mean lose? That hurts! Please, no, don't lose again!" he mocked. "Please!"

"I mean the injuries!" the voice said louder, losing patience. "Those were not coincidences. We can hurt you—bad. You better listen!"

"Look," John said. "I appreciate your psych-out efforts. Very creative. But I can't help it if we're better than you." He started to move on. "Now, if you don't mind, I have to get to school."

"You will be responsible! You better listen,"

the goalie said, "or else! Your whole team will be history."

"Why don't you go back to gardening or pruning the hedges or whatever you were doing," John said, as he continued on his way. "I guess I'll be seeing—and beating—you later, chump!" he called back over his shoulder.

The mask retreated into the bushes. John chuckled out loud. These guys were too much, he thought, shaking his head in disbelief. How pathetic that they had to resort to these ridiculous tactics.

He wasn't going to let their stupid head games bother him one bit. He would never crack. They didn't call him "Steel Wall" Stevenson for nothing. They could try to scare him all they wanted.

Just one thing nagged at him. Of all the players on the team, why did they choose to follow him around?

Two can play that game, John thought. After today's game, he'd do some following himself.

CHAPTER 7

"Hat-trick Hector!" John called, as Hector Ruiz scored his second goal of the game that day. John was pulling for Hector to score three goals in one game, so he could have the coveted nickname. "One more and you got it!"

But later on, the mean team retaliated with two goals of their own. Robbie enthusiastically snapped photos from the sidelines, and when he wasn't taking pictures, he was cheering the Penguins on. John noticed that he was clearly enjoying himself. The game was certainly action-packed.

All the Penguins were in top form today. Barry's stomach trouble, Hector's headache, and Kevin's strange paralysis were gone. The boys didn't give their injuries a second thought.

The night started to fall fast. John hated that one thing about winter. He didn't mind the cold, and he loved snow. But he hated how the daylight was sucked away just when he started to enjoy himself. It meant less ice time.

The game was tied two–two, and soon it would be impossible to see the puck.

"I call for a shoot-out," Steve announced. "It's a tie game and it's getting dark."

The mystery team looked to one another and mumbled. "Okay," Scarface said. "You're on."

John felt excitement rise in his chest. Shoot-outs were the toughest for goalies, occurring only when a game was tied and in overtime. Five players from each side took penalty shots on each goalie—one-on-one. The shots usually came rapid-fire. And a tired-out goalie had to be quick and alert, even though it was the end of the game.

The Penguins chose their five: Hector, Kevin, Barry, Steve, and Tiger. The other team had only five to offer.

They flipped a coin. The Penguins won the toss; they would go first. "Let's do it!" Steve cheered. "It's getting dark."

Hector took the puck, skated to the cutoff point, and, with a flick of his wrist, sent the puck speeding up to the left corner of the net. Scarface leapt and was able to block it in no time. He landed square on his skates, ready for the next shot.

Next, Kevin slapped one with his trademark speed. But he didn't have a lot of control on the puck, and it zoomed right toward the goalie's big, thick blade. A giveaway.

One by one, Steve shot, Tiger shot, and Barry nearly slid one in. But Scarface was on his toes. No Penguins scored.

Now it was the other team's chance. John was as ready as he would ever be, though his stomach was flip-flopping like a fish out of water. He vowed not to lose this game to a shoot-out.

Skeleton Boy shot first, and it was a close one, out of John's reach. Luckily it hit the pipe—the edge of the goal—and bounced out.

The short kid came next. He shot one wildly, so that it was completely out of bounds. That was good news for John, because he was extra ready for the next shot.

Boom—a puck came from the big kid. It was a diver—and John sprang across and whacked it with his blocker just in time. But he landed hard on his side on the solid ice.

Quickly John scrambled up to block the next shot. *Slam*—the redhead gave one right to him. John nearly laughed at his growl of frustration at the lame attempt.

There was one more shot left.

Raggedy Andy came up to the line. He took his time, no doubt trying to psych John out.

A dead silence fell on the pond. John could hear the hooting of the owls perched in the trees in the woods. Night was minutes away. It was hard to see. Luckily, Steve had put in the Day-Glo orange pucks for the shoot-out.

Come on, John thought. *I'm waiting. I'm ready.*

Raggedy Andy's white face seemed to glow in the night. He bared his rotten teeth, clenching them.

He shot.

It was high and to the right—A jump for John.

John leapt with all his might.

It was out of reach.

Thinking quickly, John thrust out his stick. It caught the orange puck on its edge. It was just the right tip.

The puck flew out of bounds.

John landed on the ice again and was surrounded by cheering Penguins.

But it was still two–two. And nighttime had arrived in full force.

"What are you cheering for? You didn't win. We have to finish," Scarface barked at Steve. "Tomorrow . . . same time . . . same place."

"Okay," Steve said.

As the team packed up, Robbie approached John. "Good game," he said earnestly. "I got some great shots of your dives. These will look great in the yearbook—next to the photos from the regular season, of course."

"Thanks," John said.

"Are you walking home?" Robbie asked. "I'll wait for you."

John ripped off his padding and stuffed it into his gear bag. "Nah, I'm going to help these guys smooth out the pond," he said, nodding toward Sanjay and Steve, who were tossing buckets of water on the pond surface. "You can go on without me," he added, remembering his plan to follow the mystery team. He was determined to find out where they go.

"Okay," Robbie answered. "You were right about those guys," he added. "Totally strange." He gave John a high five and set off down the hill toward home.

John turned to glance at the opposition across the pond. Like always, they had disappeared. He was dying to know where they always went in such a hurry.

John hung back as the Penguins started to break up. He asked Steve and Sanjay to wait around with him.

"Wait around for what?" Sanjay asked.

"Some exploration," John said, pulling a flashlight out of his gear bag. "Don't tell Mr. Waters—I borrowed this from science lab today."

69

Steve shook his head. "I don't get it. What are you up to?"

"What are *they* up to is the question," John said. "I want to know where they go after every game. Ever noticed that they're gone in a flash?"

Sanjay looked over toward the other side of the pond. "Well, there's only one place they *could* go," he said, catching on.

Steve caught on, too. "You don't mean that . . ." he said tentatively. "In the dark?"

John nodded gravely. He turned the flashlight on, illuminating the stunned expression on Steve's face. "Come on. We'll just check out their footprints, or poke around for clues, that's all."

Sanjay groaned. "I knew it. For some reason I knew we'd end up in those woods sooner or later."

Steve shook his head doubtfully. "All right, I'm game. I just hope you know what you're doing, Stevenson," he said warily.

"Don't worry," John assured him. "I'll get us in—and out—safely," he added confidently, though a trace of trepidation crept up his spine.

"Just one question," Steve asked. "How are we going to find our way once we're in there?"

John pulled out a plastic bag of small white marble chips. "I also borrowed these from Mrs. Gartner's rock garden on the way to school," he explained. "We won't make the same mistake as

Hansel and Gretel. We can mark our way with these, and the animals won't eat them."

"Now that's what I'm afraid of," Sanjay said, pulling on his jacket and zipping it up. "Animals. How do we keep them from eating *us?*"

"Good point." John paused. "I hadn't exactly thought of that . . ." he said. "We can just stay as close to the woods' edge as possible, and only investigate a little. We won't be long."

Sanjay and Steve exchanged reluctant glances.

"Come on," John insisted. "Let's go before they're too far gone."

"Okay," Steve relented.

"All right," Sanjay agreed. "But I have to be home in time for dinner or my mother will send out an APB."

The three boys left their gear bags leaning on the logs, then carefully and quietly walked around the pond to the other side. John shone his flashlight on the edge of the woods looking for a clearing. He found a small opening off to the right side.

"In here," he said. John felt a rush of excitement as he entered the thicket. Inside the woods it seemed ten times darker.

Curious, John switched off his flashlight for a few seconds. "Cool," he said. He felt like he had his eyes shut, it was so dark.

"What are you doing?" Steve asked in a panic.

"I just wanted to see how dark it was in here," John explained. He flicked the flashlight back on and shone it on the ground, frantically searching for footprints. "I guess the ground is too hard," John noted, then stamped his own foot to see if it would leave an impression. It proved his theory right. His buddies followed him as he shone the way through the woods.

"Now what?" Steve asked, his voice breaking through the crunch of their footsteps and the hoots of owls. "If we can't find footprints, then we'll never find these guys."

Sanjay held the plastic bag with the white stones, dropping one every few feet as they moved ahead. "We can still just poke around a little," he said, excited like John about the adventure.

"Yeah," John agreed. "I've never been in here before. And I've always been curious."

Steve shrugged impatiently. "I still don't think we're going to find anyth—*aaah!*" he screamed.

John whirled around. Sanjay dropped the bag of stones in shock.

"Help!" Steve called. Frantically, John shone the flashlight to locate him.

He found him clinging desperately to a tree trunk.

The tree trunk next to the hole he had fallen into.

CHAPTER 8

"Help!" Steve cried again.

John and Sanjay rushed over to grab him. Placing the flashlight on the ground so that it illuminated the area around the hole, John grabbed one of Steve's arms while Sanjay grabbed the other. They held tight with both hands, making sure they had a firm grip.

"Count of three, let go of the tree and we'll pull you out," John said, forcing composure.

"Okay," Steve answered nervously.

"Ready, Sanjay?" John asked as calmly as he could. Like on the ice, he had to focus. He had to zoom in on nothing else but pulling Steve out of the hole.

"Ready," Sanjay answered.

"One . . . two . . . three," John counted, then grunted with exertion as he and Sanjay pulled with all their might.

With another heave, John and Sanjay tumbled backward, and Steve was up and out of the hole.

Panting, John took the flashlight and shone it into the hole. It was deep—he couldn't see the bottom. He crouched carefully as he peered into the darkness. He thought he saw some tiny movement.

He did.

His flashlight illuminated hundreds of white, writhing maggots.

John scrambled back in horror.

"What?" Steve and Sanjay asked in unison. "What's in there?"

John stared at Steve, wide-eyed. He pointed at his hockey jersey, now covered with dirt—and a few squirming creatures.

"Mag—maggots," John was barely able to utter.

Steve screamed.

"Hold still," Sanjay said, keeping a cool head and picking up a stick. "Keep still and I'll get them off you."

John did his best to keep his shaking hand steady while he shone the flashlight on Steve. One by one, Sanjay brushed the maggots off his jersey with the stick.

74

"I think that's it," Sanjay said after a minute, turning Steve around to examine him, head to toe.

"Great. Can we get out of here, now?" Steve asked, fear reflected in his voice.

"Not a minute too soon," John agreed.

"I'm right behind you," Sanjay added.

They followed the short path marked by the stones out of the woods. When they exited, the threesome sighed in relief. They never thought they'd be so happy to see the pond.

They trotted over to their gear bags, which were still resting against the logs. Steve hoisted his bag over his shoulder. "That was the dumbest idea you ever had, Stevenson," he said.

"I know," John admitted sheepishly as they walked along.

"Too bad we didn't find anything but that bear hole," Sanjay said.

Steve laughed. "Bear hole? Bears don't live underground—do they?"

John shrugged. "I don't think so."

"Then why was that hole there?" Sanjay asked. "Some kind of animal had to dig it."

"It had to be a pretty large animal," John said. "Or an animal with a shovel."

Steve shuddered. "I'm just glad I was able to grab on to that tree trunk. Or I would have been maggot meat for dinner."

Dinner, John thought. "What time is it?" he asked.

"Almost seven," Steve answered.

Seven o'clock? John couldn't believe it. His father was going to have his head if he didn't get home soon.

The boys picked up their pace and said their good-byes as they went their separate ways. When John approached his house, he saw his father standing on the front porch in his ski jacket, hands on his hips.

John knew it wasn't good news.

"We—we—we just lost track of time," John stuttered to his dad when he stepped into the house. He always stuttered when he lied. "We went to grab a soda and—and I just didn't realize it was taking so long."

"You're grounded until you tell me the truth," John's father said sternly, not fooled by John's fibbing. "You know you're supposed to be home no later than six."

John hung his head. He hated lying to his father. But he knew that if he told the truth, his father would become even angrier that he'd gone into the woods.

John's father stared at him long and hard. "Go to your room," he said. "Don't come out until you're ready to talk. And grounded means no hockey—understand?"

"But, Dad!" John protested. "Tomorrow is an important game! We'll lose if I'm not there—"

"So be it," Dad answered. "There are things that are more important than your games, John."

"Like what?" John mumbled, as he turned away.

"Like following the house rules," John's dad said pointedly. "Like your family."

John stomped to his room, past Marc's woeful look from the family room. Grounded? What was he going to do about the game tomorrow if he was grounded?

He closed the door behind him and booted up his computer. He dashed off some e-mail to Steve and Sanjay.

```
To: EVENSTEVEN; SANJAYP123
From: STEELWALL


  Guys—I am in a heap of trouble for
coming home late. I hope the same
didn't happen to you. I'm sorry
about the dumb idea. I just hope I
can play tomorrow—my dad says I'm
grounded! Help!
```

John hoped they would log on before long and get his message. And hopefully they wouldn't be in as much trouble as he was. The team definitely couldn't afford to lose its three best players in one fell swoop.

He surfed the Net for a while, cruising some NHL sites and checking the scores from the previous nights' games.

John turned his head to a faint tapping on the door. "Come in," he grumbled.

Slowly Marc opened the door, his eyes as big as saucers. He held something under his shirt, and pulled it out to reveal a slice of pepperoni pizza. "I brought you this so you wouldn't starve," he whispered.

John laughed at the grease and sauce stains that covered Marc's shirt. "Thanks, dude," he said, as he grabbed the slice and bit into it with gusto.

"I'm sorry you're in trouble," Marc said quietly.

"I guess I deserve it," John responded glumly.

"Who are you supposed to play tomorrow?" Marc asked as he flopped onto John's bed.

"Good question," John said, laughing. "Just this bunch of jerks. It's important for us to beat them because they're jerks."

"But isn't it always important to win?" Marc asked.

"Yes," John answered. "Definitely. But it just feels better beating jerks than it does nice guys."

"If you can't play real hockey," Marc ventured.

"Then I can smuggle *Hockeymania* in here. If you want."

John smiled at his little brother. Though he didn't feel much like playing *Hockeymania*, he was touched by Marc's attempts to make him feel better. "Sure," he said. "If you smuggle it in I'll play one game with you. Too many and Dad will get suspicious."

"Okay," Marc whispered, putting a finger to his lips. "I'll be right back."

Later that night John lay awake in his bed, thinking about the game. He had to play in that game tomorrow. He'd apologize to Dad in the morning and tell him the truth. Dad did say that he was grounded only until he told the truth, and Dad was a man of his word.

John didn't feel the least bit tired. He'd played one game of hockey with Marc. Of course, John had won again, adding to his undefeated *Hockeymania* record. But surprisingly Marc took it like a little man. His eyes didn't well up with tears. He didn't whine, and he didn't complain. John guessed that he actually listened to him the other night and was trying hard to be a good sport.

John felt restless. He jumped out of bed and opened up his gear bag, deciding he'd put new laces on his skates or something. He turned the big bag upside down and dumped out all the contents. Out tumbled his padding, jersey, helmet, mask, gloves, and . . . a folded-up piece of paper.

John took the paper, thinking it might have been an errant homework assignment or something.

He was wrong.

When he unfolded it, threatening red scrawl jumped out at him. It read:

Dear Loser:

This is your last warning. We mean business. If you and your teammates want to live, you must throw the game tomorrow.

This is no joke.

The Winners

CHAPTER 9

John stood waiting, ready, at the goal, the mystery team coming toward him, growling and clutching their sticks like swords.

A puck came at him. He blocked it, sending it flying out of bounds.

John cheered loudly. "We won!" he screamed. "We're champions again!"

But he soon noticed that his voice was the only one raised in revelry. Suddenly everyone was gone. The mystery team, like always, was gone in a flash, but his teammates had disappeared, too.

What had happened? Where could they have gone?

John threw off his mask and searched the pond. Not a soul was around.

He skated across the pond to search for his teammates on land. But no matter how hard he tried, he couldn't get to the edge. The pond kept getting longer and wider. And John continued to push his skates with all his might.

He speed-skated, faster than he'd ever gone before, like an Olympian nearing the finish line.

That's when he spotted Marc, his little brother, standing at the edge of one side of the pond, his hands cupped around his mouth. "Come home, John!" he was calling. "Come home!"

"I'm trying," John shouted, but his voice was a whisper. John tried to shout even louder, but this time nothing came out. He skated with all his might to the edge, but the pond grew bigger, and Marc was getting farther and farther away, farther and farther until he was a tiny speck on the horizon.

Gone.

John called and called after him. "Marc! Wait! I'm coming! Don't go!" But it was no use.

He brought his sharp edges around and came to a grinding halt. He looked out at the horizon all around him.

Nothing but ice. Nothing but white.

Where was he now? How would he ever get home?

Just then the ice cracked. John pushed off and started to skate away.

But the crack grew larger and spread just as fast as John was skating.

John pushed himself harder and faster than he ever had before. He checked over his shoulder.

The crack followed him, creeping up behind him like fire.

John abruptly stopped and stood his ground, but the ice didn't cease to split. Soon his legs straddled a gorge, and before he knew it the pond opened up like the mouth of a large, hungry animal.

The pond sucked John down into the freezing water. "I want to go home!" he screamed, before he sank into the icy cold. "Please let me go home!"

John sat bolt upright in bed, a beam of sunlight hitting him square in the eye. Another nightmare—no doubt brought on by the tossing and turning he did over finding the note in his gear bag.

The note meant that when the boys were in the woods, someone was near their bags by the logs. Someone had to be watching them, then. But who and where? They hadn't seen or heard a living soul. Then again, it was so dark. . . .

Should he take this note seriously? And why was he the only one getting harassed? None of the other guys said anything about being stalked. One thing was for sure: John was getting tired of it.

John climbed out of bed and turned on his computer. He wanted to see if Steve or Sanjay had responded to his message from last night.

They had. John had mail. He clicked on the first message from SANJAYP123:

I got in trouble, too, because I was late for dinner. Luckily I thought quickly and said we lost a puck in the brush, accounting for my dirty clothes, which Mom was not excited to wash. But by the time we finished dinner, she and my dad forgot all about it. You should apologize to your dad, and if that doesn't work, beg. If that doesn't work, call me and I'll beg him for you.

Later dude,
Sanjay

John clicked on the second e-mail from EVENSTEVEN:

I was the first one home, so no sweat! I hope you can play the game tomorrow! We'll be sunk without you!

Steve

P.S. I dreamt of wriggling white maggots all night!!!!

The guys didn't mention anything about threatening notes in their gear bags. That's when it finally struck him: As goalie, John was the only one who could really control the score. One slight misstep, one imperceptible second late, and a puck could go in. That must have been it.

He clicked on a third e-mail from a name he didn't recognize: HOCKEYFAN.

We are serious. This is your last chance. Your friends will die if you win tomorrow. You know what to do.

John rubbed his eyes. A death threat? Now they were crossing the line. How in the world did they get his e-mail address? This was more than a psych-out strategy. This was downright criminal—and creepy.

John was sick of these guys, and he was sick of harassment and sick of the nightmares. He wanted them all to go away. The sooner, the better.

Today, he'd show them that John Stevenson only plays to win.

That is, if he played in the game today. He sat up in bed, realizing that he was grounded.

John stepped out from bed, planning to catch his father before he started working. He made his way to the kitchen, ready to confess.

"Morning, Son," Dad said nonchalantly behind his newspaper.

"Hi, Dad," John said softly as he sat down at the table. "I'm sorry I lied last night," he began.

"That's a good start," his dad said patiently.

John went on. "I didn't want to tell you the truth because I knew the truth would make you mad, too. I was late because I was in the woods with Steve and Sanjay. We were curious—the other team always seems to disappear after the game. We figured they always go in there. We just checked it out and lost track of time." He paused and gave his father a sincere, apologetic look. "I'm sorry, Dad."

His father's face fell. "You know those woods are incredibly dangerous!" he said.

John hung his head. "I know. I promise I won't go again. Really."

"Apology accepted," his father responded, folding up the paper. After a thoughtful moment he stood to leave, and added, "I did say that you were grounded until you told the truth. You told the truth, so you're not grounded anymore."

"Thanks!" John said. That meant he could play in the game.

"But," Dad continued, "you are on probation.

Come home when you're supposed to. Or call. I'm getting too old to put up with this worry."

"Okay, Dad," John answered, then called after him, "Thanks," though he had no idea what being "on probation" entailed.

He went back to his room to get ready for school. He couldn't wait for the day to be over so he could tell those guys off and then beat them one more time.

He especially couldn't wait to play the game.

Something told him that it was going to be more than a tiebreaker. More like a backbreaker. No matter how hard it was going to be, John was determined to do anything, anyhow, any way to make sure the Penguins didn't lose.

CHAPTER 10

John absentmindedly twirled his combination lock as he took in the early-morning chatter around him. Next to him, as usual, Andrea Jennings was chattering nonstop and wearing too much perfume. Patty Zuber, as usual, stood next to her, hanging on every word, lapping up all the gossip.

"Did you see it?" Andrea was telling Patty. "I mean, who could have done that, and why?"

"Maybe it was the Butler Valley Vikings," Patty spoke up. "Or the Plainfield Pilots."

"I guess," Andrea said. "But why would they do it now? Hockey season is over. Right, John?"

John pulled his head out of his locker and dumped his algebra book in his backpack.

"Right, John?" Andrea repeated. "Hockey season is over."

He snapped his head in Andrea's direction. He guessed they were talking to him. Usually he tuned her out in the mornings, and he wasn't used to being directly addressed by Andrea.

"Uh—yeah," John answered as he slammed his locker shut. "It's been over for weeks. Why?"

"That's why it doesn't make sense—about the trophy case," Andrea said, gleeful that she had a tidbit for John. "Why would a rival team do that if the season's been over for weeks?"

"What about the trophy case?" John asked, bewildered. He nodded in the direction of Steve and Sanjay, who were approaching him. "What's going on?" he asked when he saw their grim expressions.

"Come on," Sanjay said. "We'll show you."

John followed his best friends' quick footsteps as they led him around the corner and down the hall. John could see a crowd of students milling around the trophy case. Mr. Makepeace, the janitor, was asking kids to stand back while he went toward the case with a broom and dustpan. Principal Harris stood sadly nearby. He appeared to be on the verge of tears.

When they reached the crowd, John stood on his tiptoes and peered over the tops of the curious heads.

He opened his mouth in horror.

This time the mystery team had gone too far.

John couldn't believe what he saw. And he knew the mystery team was definitely responsible.

The trophy case had been smashed. Glass shards were scattered all over the floor in front of it. The championship trophy they had just won lay on its side in the case, the golden hockey player broken in half. And the team photo, proudly tacked up behind it, had been scribbled on in red marker. Red X's covered every smiling face in the photo. "Losers" was scrawled across the wall in red spray paint.

John recognized the scrawl from the letter he found in his gear bag.

"Do you think they did this?" Sanjay asked John.

John nodded. "No doubt. Those guys are more deranged than I thought."

"What should we do?" Steve asked. "Tell the principal? Call the cops? We don't even know who these guys are, or where they come from."

"We'll find out today," John said. "And if they keep this stuff up, we'll bring the police squad to our next game."

And John was serious. He was determined more than ever to find out just who the mystery team was.

*   *   *

The mystery team had gone too far, that was for sure, John thought as he walked down the hall.

But how would he get them to stop? Should he throw the game today like they'd been asking him to do? Would that put an end to everything? Would they go away, or keep the pond as theirs, as they had threatened?

But how could John throw a game? Letting his teammates down like that was despicable. It was like quitting.

He didn't know what to do. . . . All he did know was that he wished the mystery team would pull one of their disappearing acts—for good.

"John!" Robbie Kaplan called as John passed the yearbook office. He poked his head out of the doorway and motioned John inside. "Come here, quick!" he said excitedly. "I have something really . . . *weird* to show you."

John stopped. He was on his way to lunch, and though he was starving, figured he could spare a few minutes for Robbie.

John stepped into the yearbook office, a tiny closet of a room, full of computers and papers. Photos were tacked up on every available inch of wall space. A large table sat in the middle of the room, covered with papers and piles of old copies of *Hillville Middle Memories*.

"Have a seat," Robbie offered.

John sat, giving Robbie a curious look. "Hey, thanks for coming by yesterday," he said.

"No problem," Robbie answered. "It was fun—for me. You guys were way too intense. You didn't look like you were having fun at all."

John considered his comment. What could be more fun than playing hockey? Even if it was against a bunch of crazy brutes from nowhere. "Of course we were having fun," John said defensively. "I mean, it was different from our usual pond games, but it was still fun."

"Sure, whatever," Robbie said. "But that's not why I dragged you in here. Check this out—this is really freaky," he said eagerly. He opened up a folder that contained black-and-white photos from the previous night's game. "I just developed these," he said proudly.

"Cool shots," John said, leafing through them, and they were.

Robbie then checked the spines of the old yearbooks piled in front of him. "Our theme this year is 'Now and Then'," he explained, "and we're comparing life at Hillville Middle today to that of fifty years ago." He caught his breath as he chose *Hillville Middle Memories, 1949,* and started leafing through it.

"Listen—I didn't have much of a dinner last night," John said. Why was he here? He didn't care about the yearbook. "So I don't want to miss lunch—"

"Okay, okay," Robbie said. "I'll be quick." He stopped at a page and took a deep breath. "It didn't hit me until I had the photos from yesterday lying right next to this old book." He pushed the old yearbook toward John. "First I noticed the kid with the scar on his face. Then, on closer look, I realized that the whole team of those kids you were playing yesterday are look-alikes to the kids in here. Isn't this freaky?"

John's eyes froze on a yearbook photo of Scarface. Then his eyes moved to the five other yearbook photos around it. The page was framed by a black border. *In Memoriam* the bold type at the top of the page read.

John pulled the yearbook closer. He examined the other photos. He didn't need to compare them with Robbie's game photos. A wave of dizziness overcame him: He recognized the other five photos, too.

There, alongside Scarface, were Raggedy Andy, the big guy, the short kid, Red, and Skeleton Boy.

They looked different—cleaner and smiley and young and innocent. They were miles apart from their angry, imposing, stinking, falling-apart selves.

John read the paragraph under the headline:

Hillville Middle remembers our students who disappeared in Grant's Wood this year: Franklin Zier, Marcus Andrews, Danny Adlerman, Tony Tirello, and Robert Fullerman. They were best known as the most enthusiastic hockey players Hillville had seen in years. Though they had a 0–15 season, their winning spirits live on in our hearts forever.

John closed the yearbook, spooked.

"Am I right?" Robbie asked. "Is there a bizarre resemblance or what? I couldn't believe it when I saw this."

John was speechless. It was more than a bizarre resemblance. They were dead ringers for the mystery team. They *were* the mystery team.

"I guess they disappeared almost exactly fifty years ago today," Robbie pointed out.

Now it all started making sense to John: their out-of-date uniforms, their burning desire to win, their pale skin, decrepit odor, and decaying teeth . . . and that hole in the ground . . .

"Hey, Earth to John," Robbie was saying. "Are you all right? I mean it's just a funny coincidence, right? Or maybe the guys you play are related to—"

John stood up and ran from the yearbook office.

"Hey!" he heard Robbie calling after him. "Are you okay, man?"

John ignored Robbie's calls and ran down the hallway in a panic.

He burst into the boys' room. His stomach lurched. Suddenly he didn't feel hungry anymore. He splashed his face with cold water and stared at it in the mirror.

Could it be possible? John thought things like this happened only on cheesy late-night movies.

Have they been playing hockey with a team of the undead?

CHAPTER
11

John felt like a freaked-out zombie for the rest of the day. He went through the motions of going to class, and appeared to pay attention, but he was really thinking about what had happened in the yearbook room.

In algebra, his last class, his eyes were glued to the clock. He went through the rote motions of opening his book and pretending to solve word problems, but John needed to solve his own problems right now. He tried to sort through what he had just found out. His stomach felt like a hockey puck was bouncing around in it as he pieced his discovery together.

The mystery team—they weren't lying. They *were* from Hillville. They had played on that same pond half a century before John and his buddies.

They were the six students who'd disappeared in the woods fifty years ago—all "enthusiastic" members of the hockey team who had probably played hard but never won a game.

And now, somehow, for some reason, they'd crawled out of their maggot-ridden graves in the woods—where Steve had fallen—and they wanted to take the title of champions.

How could winning be so important to the dead? John thought. What did it matter? And why did they wait fifty years? Was that a magic number? Or were they waiting for the ultimate challenge—a team undefeated, to their unvictorious bunch?

John shuddered suddenly, thinking of being trapped in an undead limbo, simply because he wanted to win a game. He enjoyed winning, but, as his dad had said, weren't there more important things in life?

Would he, too, take his competitive edge to the grave? John wondered. Because they died young, had they died one-dimensional—all about hockey—and not much else? Would that happen to John, or would his life be longer, fuller, and about much more? It was a question he would have laughed at a day ago. But now it seemed important.

All of those warnings. *Like an idiot,* John thought, *I ignored them.* They were serious. *Dead serious.*

And John had no choice. He had to throw the game today.

They would lose pond rights. But John didn't care anymore. It suddenly didn't seem so important, compared to the life-and-death situation in his hands right now.

It was do or die.

It would be easy to do. But he couldn't be obvious about it. And he couldn't start screwing up the second he got out on the ice. No, then Steve would yank him out of the game.

He had to let the guys down without letting them know he was letting them down, because if they lived through the game, John didn't want his buddies to blame him.

Somehow he had to convince them that he was trying his best, while allowing one too many pucks to slide through the goal.

But what if the Penguins scored wildly today? John shook the thought out of his mind. No matter what, they had to lose.

He glanced at the clock on the wall once more. He felt like the school day would never end.

Something else nagged at him. He remembered cockily challenging the mystery team after each game. Could this have been avoided if he hadn't egged them on? And if he had taken their warnings seriously, would the trophy case be ruined?

Would his teammates' lives still be in danger?

When John met up with Steve and Sanjay to walk to the pond, he felt like he was walking to his own death.

"Hey, man," Sanjay said. "What's with you today? You've been acting weird all day."

"Yeah," Steve agreed. "Was it because you got in trouble last night? Or did the trophy case freak you out?"

"Nah," John said. "I just . . ." he didn't know what to say without sounding like a head case. He didn't want to say he didn't feel good—then Steve might not put him in. He certainly didn't want to tell them the truth. "I've just been gearing up for the game, that's all."

Steve pumped a fist into the air. "We'll show 'em! And they better keep their promise. After we smear them today, we better not see their ugly faces around ever again."

"Yeah!" Sanjay agreed. "We'll get our pond— and our peace—back. I can't wait to get back to playing our normal scrimmages."

"Yeah," John mumbled, suddenly feeling nostalgic for the carefree, fun games they used to play. Funny, didn't Robbie say that they didn't look like they were having fun? Now that John thought back on it, Robbie might be right. "You said it Sanjay," he agreed. "I am so sick of these guys."

As a matter of fact, that wasn't the only thing he was sick of, John thought. Though John loved hockey, he was sick of it now. He was sick of the competition. He was sick of all the killer exertion.

He was especially sick of the head games, the nightmares, and the pressure and worry that were plaguing him now.

None of it was fun—at all.

"I was thinking up some strategies last night," Steve was saying. "I want to try a diamond or a box formation, even though we won't be in a power-play situation. I think it would pay off anyway."

"You sound like Coach Ramirez," Sanjay said.

"Yeah," John added quickly. This was not the time for Steve's hardcore strategies. "Why don't we save that stuff for the regular season? It takes all the fun out of the game. Why don't we just play like always?"

Steve shot John a funny look. "You do want to win, don't you? You do want the pond back, right? Or have you forgotten who came up with this stupid bet in the first place, Mr. Competition?"

"Of course I want to win!" John said, maybe a

little too enthusiastically. "I mean . . . why wouldn't I? I was just saying that we shouldn't have to be so structured, that's all."

John realized he had to keep his mouth shut. He *had* proposed the wager. The whole mess was his fault. He wondered if his competitive drive had made a mess of everything, or if the Hillville Penguins of 1949 would have come after them anyway.

John sighed. He had no way of knowing. All he did know was that each Penguin—new or old—was going to be playing his heart out today.

As if his life depended on it.

CHAPTER 12

When they arrived at the pond, John's nerves grew worse. He felt his breath shorten as he sat on the end of a log, pulling out his padding from his gear bag. Looking at the mystery team now freaked him out more than ever. He felt their dagger-stares coming from all sides.

Steve stormed over to the mystery team to confront them. "That was lame—what you did to our trophy case. Why don't you grow up and play like real hockey players," he said.

The mystery team just snickered.

"We have no idea what you're talking about," Raggedy Andy mocked, while his teammates snickered some more.

Sanjay came up behind Steve. "You know what

we're talking about," he added, "And you're lucky we didn't tell the police."

The team laughed even louder this time.

Steve pulled Sanjay aside. "There's no point trying to talk to these losers," Steve said. "We'll just have to teach them a lesson on the ice."

They walked back to their side of the pond. Steve herded everyone together and clapped to get their attention. "Okay, guys," he said. "This is the tiebreaker. Don't forget—these are the nitwits that vandalized our trophy case," he said angrily. "We can't let them get away with that. We've got to win this game. Let's show them that we're champions, no matter what they smash or scribble on!"

"Yeah!" the Penguins shouted.

Great, John thought, trying his best to muster enthusiasm. *Now they're more determined than ever to win.* He felt sick. How was he ever going to get through this game?

"Let's crush 'em!" Sanjay hollered, rallying the team some more. "In cold blood!"

"Enough with the cheerleading," the big guy from the mystery team called over. "Are we going to play or shake our pom-poms?"

"Okay," Steve answered. "We're ready."

Ready as I'll ever be, John thought, as he skated over to take his position at the goal. He quickly went over his own strategy in his head. He had to hold them for the first half of the game. Then, after break, he'd slip up. But all of that depended on if—and how much—his own team was scoring.

He hated thinking this way, but he had no choice.

"Face off!" Paul Linder called, dropping the puck.

Red and Steve went at it, slicing up the ice as if it were a piece of pie.

Steve quick-flicked the puck to Kevin. Instantly Kevin took a long one-timer.

John winced. *Not so soon!* he silently pleaded.

He got his wish. Kevin missed. The Penguins of 1949 now had the puck.

The skeletal blond kid came racing toward John in a breakaway. Nothing stood between him and the goal except for John.

The skeleton shot, quick as a sniper. John effortlessly deflected the puck, but the deadly glare Skeleton Boy gave him made him uneasy.

Yeah, they think I'm crazy, John thought. He shuddered inside. Blocking the puck was a natural reaction—a reflex. Goofing up—and losing—was going to be harder than he thought.

By the first break, John was an emotional wreck. There was no score, and both teams were playing like fierce pagan warriors. John blocked about ten shots, and with each one came a burning in the pit of his stomach. With each save also came death-glares from the opposition.

Don't worry guys, he told them mentally. *You'll get your win. You'll get your glory.*

Big deal. It was odd, John thought, that winning, something that was so important to him once, just didn't seem so important anymore.

Steve gathered everyone as they sipped water and juice. "Come on," he urged. "We have to score! What's going on, guys?"

"It's just impossible to get anything past that goalie today," Kevin said. "I can't get anything even close—even on breakaway. And forget about decoying—he's got my number now."

"Good thing we have Steel Wall," Paul said, patting John on the shoulder. "Good work, man."

"Thanks," John mumbled. And he deserved the praise. He had played hard. He'd blocked everything that came near him. But the show was over. Now it was time for him to save their lives.

"Okay," Steve called, signaling from the pond. "Back on the ice."

John skated to the net. It was now or never.

The face-off brought the puck to Scarface's territory. And John's Penguins were getting antsy, he could tell. They were shooting like they were at a carnival gallery, aiming at mechanical ducks.

But nothing got past Scarface.

The Penguins remained relentless. It was as if

they weren't going to leave Scarface's realm until they scored a goal.

The puck stayed down at the other side for a while. Normally, John would have welcomed the break. But now it was different. Now he was fretting.

The sun was sinking lower in the sky. Soon John had to make his move. *If* he ever got the chance. The Penguins were hotter than ever.

Steve passed to Sanjay. Sanjay tipped to Kevin. Kevin flipped to Hector. Hector slid to Barry. They had such fantastic, quick control that the mystery team lunged, fell, checked, slapped, and scraped, but they couldn't get ahold of the puck.

John knew what they were trying to do. They were trying to wear the other team down—exhaust them so they could catch them when they were weak.

It was working. And the mystery team was getting angrier and angrier by the second.

Finally, Hector shot.

The puck rose at a perfect angle, making a beeline for a hole in the upper-right-hand corner of the net.

Scarface leapt. He threw out his stick.

It looked like it was in. John squeezed his eyes shut. He didn't want to see it.

But he could tell from the familiar groans of his teammates that it didn't happen.

John snapped open his eyes. Finally, the opposition had control of the puck. *It's about time,* John groused silently.

But the Penguins were fast. They sped to their side and formed a diamond defense in a flash.

Now's the time, John thought, as he saw Red racing toward him with the puck. John could tell he was just itching to shoot. *Just do it,* he mentally begged.

He did. The shot came off to the left, on the outside. John prepared to dive. He'd take a leap just a little too late. . . .

The puck zoomed forward.

This is it, John thought, his heart racing, his stomach tightening.

He was ready. He crouched, prepared to flub the game. He was set to miss the puck by just a few centimeters. He was just about to dive . . . when out of nowhere, Sanjay thrust his stick out right in front of him, sweeping the puck out of bounds. "Thought I'd help you out a little, buddy," he said, giving John the thumbs-up.

"Good defense!" Steve shouted. "Keep it up, guys! Help our Steel Wall out! Don't even let them get near him!"

No! John screamed to himself. *Just stay out of my way! Please!* They didn't know what they were doing. They didn't know that their lives were on the line.

John started to shake inside. It was getting later and dimmer. He knew he shouldn't have waited so long.

Soon they'd be out of light. And the game would still be tied. Did these ghouls count a tie as a win or a loss? he wondered.

It didn't matter. John didn't want to have to go through with this all over again.

There was no way he was going to let that happen.

Raggedy Andy had the puck now. He slapped it hard.

John barely saw it coming. Before he knew it, it bounced right off his shin guard. No score.

"Quick thinking!" Steve cheered. "Go Steel Wall!"

It was an accident. And time was running out. He needed just one more chance.

He got it.

The big kid had possession now. He came around back, passing it quickly to Red, who was waiting midpond.

At lightning speed, Red drove the puck straight down the middle, feathering through the ten legs and five sticks of the Penguins.

Though his teammates missed it, it looked like an easy block for John, heading right for his five-hole.

But he didn't care.

This one was going in, no matter what.

It came straight to John. He saw someone skating fiercely toward it.

Sanjay. Again.

No! John pleaded. *Don't!*

Sanjay was too late. John faked a slip. He fell over the puck. After a heart-wrenching second, he scrambled up.

It was in.

Score: Hillville Penguins 1949: 1

       Hillville Penguins 1999: 0

CHAPTER 13

The roars and cheers of the 1949 Penguins boomed across the pond. John thought the ice would shatter from the noise.

He breathed a deep sigh of relief, but then felt a stab in his chest when he noticed the disappointed expressions of his teammates and the slow, knowing nod of Scarface across the pond.

John pulled his mask up. "I don't know how it happened—" he started, only half-feigning disappointment. He did feel bad.

"Don't worry about it," Steve said. "We still have a little time. We'll score, right guys?"

"Right!" the Penguins chimed in.

"Please, no," John muttered to himself. He felt bad enough letting one puck in. He didn't want to have to do it again. And he certainly couldn't handle a sudden-death overtime—literally or figuratively. He just wanted to call it quits—skate off the ice, go home, and crawl into a fetal ball.

But he couldn't. He had to play the few remaining minutes of the game. Luckily it would be just that—minutes—because darkness started to drape the sky.

Steve dug out a bright orange puck from his gear bag, and was in a hurry to get back into play.

Face off! The Penguins 1999 took the puck immediately. They sped toward the goal, the puck in the capable control of Barry Sears.

But abruptly Barry faltered. John couldn't see why—no one was near him. Then Steve fell. And Sanjay. And Hector and Kevin.

The puck flew astray as little holes of ice seemed to pop open and tug each player in by the leg. It looked like some kind of monster was pulling them down into the freezing water.

Quickly the boys scrambled, pulling their legs out, floundering and slipping on the ice.

"Game over!" John called in a panic as he skated over to help his friends. He knew that the mystery team somehow caused the ice to break, probably because Barry was getting too close to scoring. "Game over! You win. We lose. You can have this stinking pond!"

John helped his teammates to their side of the pond, then frantically dug into their gear bags for towels. He, Tiger, Pete, and Paul wrapped their shivering teammates' legs as the 1949 Penguins cheered in victory.

"Well," Steve said, his teeth chattering. "I guess the season's over anyway. The ice is thinning."

"Yeah," John said. "I guess so."

"I don't know about you guys, but that was scary. I felt like I was being pulled under the ice," Kevin added.

"You must be delirious," John said. "From all the exertion."

"By the way, great game, guys," Steve chimed in.

"I think that was the best game we ever played," Sanjay pointed out. "Even if we did lose."

Winners. Losers. John just didn't care anymore. And his teammates seemed to be taking the loss pretty well. He felt relieved, glad the nightmare was over.

He turned to get a last look at the antique Penguins. But, as usual, they were nowhere to be found.

"I hope we don't see their ugly mugs anymore," Sanjay said, noticing John's glance. "Now that they've won."

"Well, I guess we gave up the pond, so if we're

men of our words then we shouldn't come here anymore," Barry said.

"We are men of our words," Steve agreed. "And good sports. And real champions. They can have this pond. There are others."

"Or we could play in-line hockey," John pointed out, though he was looking forward to taking a nice, long break from his former favorite sport. "We can play that all year round."

The group packed up, the wet players anxious to get home and into dry clothes. "Go on ahead," John told Steve and Sanjay. "You guys are wet. I just want to mellow out for a few minutes."

Steve and Sanjay exchanged curious looks. "You're not thinking of going into the woods again, are you?"

"No way," John assured them. "Just go ahead. I'll leave before it gets too dark."

They shrugged and went on their way, as John leaned against a log and watched their figures grow smaller and smaller, then blend into the inky night.

When they were no longer in sight, John opened his gear bag and pulled out a heavy black ink marker. He grabbed a nearby stone and placed it on his lap as he wrote: *In Memoriam: Hillville Penguins 1949. Record: 1–15.*

John rose, then carefully walked to the other side of the pond. He knelt and placed the stone where the mystery team would gather. "Congratulations," John said. "You finally won."

He stood, dusted off his knees, and stopped short when he saw movement in the pond.

Squinting in the night, John could have sworn he saw six figures swimming in the freezing water, under the ice. Briefly he made out their tattered uniforms. But as he watched icy bubbles float to the surface, they disappeared.

"Now you can rest in peace," John whispered.

John trekked home, numb, as if he had been taking a swim in the frigid pond water.

As he loped down the dark streets of his neighborhood, John tried to figure everything out. The Penguins of 1949 had some unfinished business, he realized. His team played sixteen games in a season. The old yearbook said that the '49 Penguins were 0–15. They never got to play the final game. And they never got to win.

They must have craved the ultimate game, stopping at nothing—dirty play, vandalism—to encourage the utmost competition in John and the guys. They wanted to win against the team who wanted to beat them more than anything.

They crawled out, in their undead states, from under the pond through the hole—or grave—in the woods, so as not to break the icy pond surface. In the end, they destroyed the ice so there would be no question of a rematch; and no question of John and his buddies returning.

And there *was* no question. John was looking forward to *not* playing hockey for a while. Maybe he'd get into reading comic books with Robbie Kaplan.

When John approached his doorstep, he never thought he'd seen a more welcome sight. Home, sweet home. Somehow, he knew he'd get a good night's sleep tonight.

When he opened the door, Marc scrambled to the doorway to greet him. "Hey!" he said. "Did you win?"

"Yeah," John said happily. "We won." At least he considered staying alive a definite win. He ruffled Marc's hair and turned to go in his room.

But he turned back. "How about some *Hockeymania?*" he asked Marc.

Marc's face brightened like a new morning sun. "Yeah!" was his enthusiastic response.

As they played, John enjoyed looking at Marc's changing face: determination to glee to solid concentration. He hoped Marc wouldn't get as caught up in game-playing and game-winning as John had. Somehow John would do his best to make sure that didn't happen.

Marc's Wayne Gretzky shot at John's goal.

John reacted just a hair slower than usual.

115

Marc's puck went into the net just as the buzzer went off.

"Hey!" Marc cried incredulously, his eyes widening in surprise. "I can't believe it! I won!"

"You certainly did," John said proudly. "You beat me fair and square."

Just then Dad stepped into the room. "What's all the commotion about?" he asked. "Did somebody win the lottery?"

"Dad! I beat John at *Hockeymania.*" Marc told him. "I won! I'm champion!"

"Congratulations," Dad said, giving John a knowing wink.

John smiled as he hoisted Marc upon his shoulders. "It was a tough game," he said.

That was two losses for him tonight, John mused. But Marc's beaming face, and the knowledge that his teammates returned from the game tonight unharmed, made John feel like he was the champion of the world.

EPILOGUE: THE MIDNIGHT SOCIETY

John and his friends never did return to the pond near Grant's Wood. But they did get into in-line hockey—after taking a break for the rest of the winter.

And John continued to play sports, though he took them just a little less seriously now. Suddenly being champion wasn't what the game was all about anymore. And he vowed that no matter what the sport, the minute it stopped being fun would be the minute he'd stop playing.

Marc now had the confidence to become really good at Hockeymania, and he started to beat John in his own right—fair and square.

John decided that he could use some time on the sidelines, and he thought to combine his sports know-how with something noncompetitive, like writing. With Robbie's encouragement, he contributed to the school paper and even the yearbook sports section.

The memory of the 1949 Hillville Penguins lingered in John's mind, but he was glad that it was only that—a memory. He no longer received unexpected visits in the night, nor threatening letters or e-mail. Life went completely back to normal for John Stevenson.

For now.

So, you liked this creepy sports story? Well, you can come back for more anytime. We're always here, at midnight, around the campfire—if you ever find your way back.

Oh, and be careful on your way home.

It's very dark out.

I declare this meeting of the Midnight Society closed.

ABOUT THE AUTHOR

K. S. RODRIGUEZ has written over a dozen books for young readers, including the two original *Dawson's Creek* stories *Long Hot Summer* and *Major Meltdown,* and *Dawson's Creek: The Official Scrapbook.* Her hobbies include reading, cooking, traveling, playing the piano, and socializing. Ms. Rodriguez lives in Manhattan with her husband, Ronnie.

It's tough being the new kid on the planet.

the journey of
ALLEN
STRANGE™

Turn the page for a sneak peek
at a new Nickelodeon series
available January 1999 from Minstrel Books
Published by Pocket Books

Monday, 4:27 A.M., PDT
200 Miles Beyond Earth's Atmosphere

The planet spun like a cotton-flecked balloon sailing through uncountable stars. A thousand strands of glittering diamonds webbed across one particular continent, clumping here and there to form cities lit bright in the darkness of night. A fiery halo crawled over the globe's eastern curve, speeding dawn across the land at a thousand miles per hour.

The alien spacecraft dropped silently through the atmosphere, skipping without resistance through the wispy upper airs. Appearing smooth from a distance, the hull was composed of flexible nested rings that shifted as they spun. Powered by alien light-energy, the craft deflected the invisible radar eyes that scanned the skies from below. The beings inside the craft wanted only to find a secluded spot to recharge before continuing their star-hopping journey. This planet was a pit stop for the travelers.

4:31 A.M.
Delport, California

Huge energy pressure waves from the descending spacecraft played havoc with the electrical fields whispering through the town. Sparks leaped crazily from power poles, grass and leaves shuddered in an invisible wind, and in one gray-and-white house all the clocks lost track of time. Glowing numerals on bedside alarm clocks now flashed 12:00 . . . 12:00 . . . 12:00 . . .

4:33 A.M.
Near Delport

"Bruce, you out there?" The dispatcher's voice crackled out of the police car speaker.

The Highway Patrol officer's eyes flicked from the dirt road to his dashboard radio. His shift was almost over, and his patrol had been quiet and uninterrupted. He reached over and thumbed the microphone. "Morning, Susie. Thought I was gonna go the whole night without hearing from you." His headlights slid over sagebrush and scrub oak as he guided his police cruiser around a curve on the back country road.

"No such luck," the drawling voice on the radio shot back. "Old Mrs. Henson just called. Said she saw some lights flashing on her property. Claims the cows are going crazy."

Bruce chuckled. Mrs. Henson called a couple of times a month. Sometimes he thought the old woman regarded his stops at her remote farm more as visits than investigations. "Somehow," he sighed, "I don't think it's the cows."

In a converted van a couple of miles away, an eavesdropper monitored their conversation. Phil Berg, self-appointed "alien hunter" and host of the *Watch the Skies* Public Access TV show, listened with half an ear to his headphones as he rummaged around for a snack. Second-hand and rewired electronic equipment lined one wall of the van, while the rest of the vehicle was littered with junk food wrappers, science fiction paperbacks, and UFO research newsletters. Under a pile of "Flying Saucer Alerts" faxes, Phil finally found an open bag of candy corn. Halloween was long past but a quick sniff of the nose detected no reason to reject the snack. It wouldn't have mattered. When Phil was extra-terrestrial hunting, anything was edible. A nearby glass of double-sugar-double-caffeine cola bore bubbling witness to this.

"Did she say where she saw these lights?" Bruce was asking his dispatcher.

She laughed. "It's on Carbon Canyon. Just off the 116."

Phil perked up. Carbon Canyon was the perfect landing place for an alien craft—rural and secluded, with fields to mark with crop circles and cattle to sample. Better than that, it was near enough that Phil could be there with his equipment and cameras if the sighting panned out. He turned up the gain on his scanner.

4:34 A.M.
Carbon Canyon

Bruce eased his cruiser onto an old wooden bridge spanning Carbon Canyon Creek and blinked in surprise at the brilliant blue light glaring from beyond the wooded hillside. The Henson farm was the only dwelling nearby, but old lady Henson owned nothing that could pump out *that* kind of wattage.

So where was the light coming from?

The hairs along the nape of Bruce's neck rose as if he were standing near an electric generator. The air smelled of ozone. Furrowing his brow in suspicion, he flicked a switch and turned on the red and blue flashers on his car roof. But he didn't turn on his siren. No, he wanted to sneak up on whoever . . . or whatever . . . was causing the unearthly glare. He brought his cruiser to a quiet stop and hopped out to investigate. He ran through the brush toward the light, cleared the trees—and stopped dead in his tracks.

Beyond the low ridge, Carbon Canyon Creek widened into a quiet pool where Bruce used to swim with his friends as a boy. But it wasn't casual midnight swimmers that skittered across the water's surface now.

A group of luminous figures floated gently above the pool. Although vaguely human-shaped, the figures shifted and shimmered without solid substance and trailed clouds of flitting light particles as they moved. A column of sparkling blue light rose up from the water, and another glowing figure within was descending gently down to hover near the others. Bruce tried to do a quick count of them—three . . . five . . . More? Less? He couldn't be sure. He was having enough trouble just trying to keep calm.

Slowly Bruce glanced upward, afraid of finding out where the strange blue light-column was coming from, but wanting to know all the same. He discovered a massive wheel of lights hovering high over the pond, made up of dark spokes and bright, sparkling spaces. The darker dividers all extended out from a smaller central opening—the source of the column.

With sickening terror, Bruce realized he was looking at a spaceship.

4:36 A.M.
Inside the Spacecraft

Light-bodies drifted through the central passage-way of the great ship. The alien crew, tired from their interstellar traveling, zipped out to refresh themselves in the lush bioenergies of the planet. For a brief moment the corridor was clear, and a smaller light-body popped its head out of a service bay. It looked both ways and, judging that it was safe to leave it's hiding place, sped down toward the alien planet below. Expressing itself more in energy than in sound waves, the stowaway's "Whee!" adequately conveyed the thrill it felt in sneaking down to see a brand new world.

The little figure flashed down the blue beam, angling sharply before hitting the water to zip toward some nearby trees. Comfortably hidden behind a live oak, the small light-body savored the strange flavors in the unfamiliar air.

4:37 A.M.
Carbon Canyon

Bruce automatically reached for his RF shoulder mike. "Susie! Susie! Come in, Susie!" he whispered, frantically pushing the transmit button.

The dispatcher's voice came through a storm of static. "What's going on, Bruce? Are you okay?"

Sparks leaped from the microphone to Bruce's hand, breaking the connection and zapping the officer's fingers. He fumbled and dropped the device, but caught it in time and pushed the button again and again.

"Bruce, come in!" Susie's call was barely audible through all the static. It rose in pitch, hissing and crackling.

Bruce couldn't be sure if she could hear him now or not. "Susie," he whispered, "there's a ship! There's lights . . . it's moving . . . it's . . . it's . . ." He could hardly breathe, realizing that he was alone and possibly in danger. But he couldn't move from the spot.

Not far away, the static was affecting Phil Berg's equipment, too. His hands flew across his instrument board, turning knobs and engaging filters in a frantic attempt to get a clear origin for the broadcast. He knocked over his soda without noticing, his heart racing with excitement and frustration. He desperately wished he could be driving to the landing site, but he couldn't until he got a firm fix recorded.

His spilled soda puddled along the work shelf, seeping through ill-fitted component covers and into the delicate electronics behind them. Concentrating on isolating Bruce's conversation, Phil pinched the fingers of one hand around a filter control knob while the fingers of his other hand grasped the knob of another console. In that split second, the spilled soda hit live wires, sending thousands of volts charging through his body. Phil squealed, his eyes bugging out and his ears smoking as the current headed for ground.

By the pond, one of the strange light-bodies drifted directly toward Bruce, almost with a sense of curiosity. Then the light creature stiffened in alarm and, faster than seemed possible, fled back to the column of blue light and vanished upward. Instantly, smaller golden columns of light descended to envelop the other alien visitors, snatching them back up into their ship. A sense of alarm and danger filled the night air.

A blast of wind from the alien ship engines hit Bruce, and he automatically brought his arm up to shield his eyes from the light above as it started to grow brighter and brighter. Terror gave movement back to his feet, and he scrambled over the hill and back to his car where he snatched up his CB radio mike. "Susie! Susie!" he yelled over the rising whine. "Come in, *please!*"

Susie's voice shouted back, "Bruce, what's going on out there?"

Bruce wanted to answer, but his jaw grew slack as he looked up. The alien ship was majestically gliding past, right over his car! His eyes watered as he watched ring structures retract and reconfigure. The thing was going to take off, and the force of the engines would blast right down on him! "Oh my—!" He dived back into his car and covered his head with his arms, ignoring Susie's frantic call.

"Bruce? Are you out there? Are you okay?"

A hurricane formed around the cruiser, wildly spinning dirt, leaves, and even rocks up and away from the spacecraft. The light outside, already blinding, grew impossibly brighter and brighter. The pressure waves rose to a subsonic roar more felt than heard. The cruiser began rocking with the pulses, its front and back bumpers alternating as they slammed repeatedly into the ground. The windshield bent inward like plastic sheeting, sending Bruce diving for cover under the dashboard.

The tires—top-of-the-line steel-belted radials—blew out like cheap balloons. The windshield flexed again, then burst into countless pieces, spraying the interior with rounded particles of safety glass.

Just when Bruce thought that the next invisible assault would stomp him and his car flat, the huge alien ship became a streak in the sky, leaving darkness and sudden silence below.

Moving slowly and carefully, Bruce peeked over the dashboard and through the shattered windshield. Carbon Canyon Creek was as quiet and serene as if nothing had happened. The only sound was Susie's voice as she continued to call desperately, "Are you okay? Bruce, what's going on out there? Come in!"

A faint glow caught the officer's attention. On the far side of the pond, peering around a tree, a luminous face stared up at the sky with unmistakable grief. Bruce blinked twice to clear his vision and looked again. The face was gone from the tree, but a sparkling trail of light was weaving its way through the bushes until it vanished into the darkness.

The dispatcher's voice was still going. "Bruce, do you need backup?"

Bruce hauled himself up to a sitting position, his hands shaking as he answered, "No. No backup. A ship . . . huge . . . lights . . . they were alive . . . one was left behind . . ."

In the *Watch the Skies* van, Phil Berg picked himself up off the floor. He had a fanatical grin plastered across his face. It was real. It was here. And he'd gotten it on tape.

And there was one left behind—for him to hunt.

The Journey of Allen Strange™

A new series of books, one every other month

It's tough being the new kid on the planet!

THE JOURNEY OF ALLEN STRANGE™

Meet Allen Strange. He's a typical teenager trying to fit in at a new school...except Allen's an alien who was accidentally stranded on Earth. Now, with the help of his new friends, Robbie and Josh Stevenson, he's trying to find a way to get home—and to keep his special powers a secret!

Based on the hit series from Nickelodeon

Original stories available in mid-January '99

A MINSTREL® BOOK
Published by Pocket Books

To find out more about The Journey of Allen Strange or any other Nickelodeon show, visit Nickelodeon Online on America Online (Keyword: NICK) or on the Web at nick.com.

2035

Read Books. Earn Points. Get Stuff!

NICKELODEON® and MINSTREL® BOOKS

Now, when you buy any book with the special Minstrel® Books/Nickelodeon "Read Books, Earn Points, Get Stuff!" offer, you will earn points redeemable toward great stuff from Nickelodeon!

Each book includes a coupon in the back that's worth points. Simply complete the necessary number of coupons for the merchandise you want and mail them in. It's that easy!

Nickelodeon Magazine.	4 points
Twisted Erasers	4 points
Pea Brainer Pencil	6 points
SlimeWriter Ball Point Pen	8 points
Zzand	10 points
Nick Embroidered Dog Hat	30 points
Nickelodeon T-shirt	30 points
Nick Splat Memo Board	40 points

- Each book is worth points (see individual book for point value)
- Minimum **40** points to redeem for merchandise
- Choose anything from the list above to total at least 40 points. Collect as many points as you like, get as much stuff as you like.

What? You want more?!?!
Then Start Over!!!

NICKELODEON/MINSTREL BOOKS POINTS PROGRAM

Official Rules

1. HOW TO COLLECT POINTS

Points may be collected by purchasing any book with the special Minstrel®/Nickelodeon "Read Books, Earn Points, Get Stuff!" offer. Only books that bear the burst "Read Books, Earn Points, Get Stuff!" are eligible for the program. Points can be redeemed for merchandise by completing the coupons (found in the back of the books) and mailing with a check or money order in the exact amount to cover postage and handling to Minstrel Books/Nickelodeon Points Program, P.O. Box 7777-G140, Mt. Prospect, IL 60056-7777. Each coupon is worth points. (See individual book for point value.) Copies of coupons are not valid. Simon & Schuster is not responsible for lost, late, illegible, incomplete, stolen, postage-due, or misdirected mail.

2. 40 POINT MINIMUM

Each redemption request must contain a minimum of 40 points in order to redeem for merchandise.

3. ELIGIBILITY

Open to legal residents of the United States (excluding Puerto Rico) and Canada (excluding Quebec) only. Void where taxed, licensed, restricted, or prohibited by law. Redemption requests from groups, clubs, or organizations will not be honored.

4. DELIVERY

Allow 6-8 weeks for delivery of merchandise.

5. MERCHANDISE

All merchandise is subject to availability and may be replaced with an item of merchandise of equal or greater value at the sole discretion of Simon & Schuster.

6. ORDER DEADLINE

All redemption requests must be received by January 31, 1999, or while supplies last. Offer may not be combined with any other promotional offer from Simon & Schuster. Employees and the immediate family members of such employees of Simon & Schuster, its parent company, subsidiaries, divisions and related companies and their respective agencies and agents are ineligible to participate.

COMPLETE THE COUPON AND MAIL TO
NICKELODEON/MINSTREL POINTS PROGRAM
P.O. BOX 7777-G140
MT. PROSPECT, IL 60056-7777

NICKELODEON

MINSTREL° BOOKS

NAME_____

ADDRESS_____

CITY _____ STATE _____ ZIP _____

THIS COUPON WORTH FIVE POINTS
Offer expires January 31, 1999

I have enclosed _____coupons and a check/money order (in U.S. currency only) made payable to "Nickelodeon/Minstrel Books Points Program" to cover postage and handling.

❑ 40–75 points (+ $3.50 postage and handling)

❑ 80 points or more (+ $5.50 postage and handling)

1464-01(2of2)